DRY WORLD

Dylan James Brock

Dry World

GenZ Publishing

2016® Dylan James Brock

GenZPublishing.org

Aberdeen, NJ

ISBN:9780692650059

For Joanna

Chapter 1

Omniscience of Adolescence

I was born in 1980, in Roosevelt City, Michigan. My father was an angry, tightly wound person, a man of contrasts – dark rage and lightning charm. Looking at our family photos you'll notice his scowl, wrenching his jowls into furrows of consternation. His father was an engineer and an executive, and my paternal great-grandmother spent most of her life in the mental hospital where she died. At twenty-one my father married a girl from the North Shore of Chicago. The daughter of a Miracle Mile ad exec and granddaughter of an airline founder. My mother once posed for an ad with me, baby John, swaddled in her arms, and any resemblance of the insurance billboard to Botticelli's Madonna was surely not coincidental, though appreciated by only a few weirdos. Good taste could be a mental illness if a diagnostic manual were written about the people of my hometown.

After elementary school my mother abandoned me to finish her education. Forgive my hyperbole; she never really left. Nevertheless, the idea that she might want to pursue a career beyond the rearing of me and my two brothers seemed as threatening as divorce and undeniably more real, and even with the onset of my smashing scholastic career, I was forced to admit that her motherly role was a Soviet globe, evidence of a time when the world was binary.

My elder brother Paul, whom my father beat so hard and so often that to punch him now is to make him laugh, turned around and pummeled me from the start: his way of welcoming me home from the hospital was to sit on my face with rubber underwear until I turned lavender and my mother pulled him off. He made me, in the fullness of his cruelty, better at taking punches from those I love. Paul had blond waves, an olive complexion, and perfect pitch. He played every instrument in our house, five, by the time he was five. He peaked at twelve, when his discovery of marijuana and alcohol opened the vat of weak acid that would slowly decay him from without. Yet the handcuffed beat downs and the pulled butcher knives were rare. As violent as our little world might sound, the darkness was only intermittent.

Somehow while Paul, my father and I were going mad, we agreed to spare our younger brother George of everything that was done to us and that we had done to each other. So George grew into a decent but benign eccentric.

But before that, before we imploded, I grew – a moody, sickly child in a whipsaw world of read-aloud fantasies, fine sand, beech trees, loyal dogs, lake vistas, constant quarrels, paper-mill odors, redlined segregation, murdered foxes, and let's not forget that man down Cherry Orchard Lane who killed his parents and himself. Of course we forgot. Honey sun blinded us all to evil. Around me, parent's estate was a kind of private universe of green dunes rolling within and beyond their property line, Rook National Park.

From unfashionable lesbian teachers to inscrutable Jungian therapists, seemingly every adult I met praised me. Reclusive scholars called me brilliant in letters to the editor. Ruined single mothers made me fudge. He, my vibrantly vicious father, took me to have my head shrunk before I had hair under my arms. I was insane because I dared to bring up all the incidents when we had hurt each other, incidents he and my mother insisted had never happened. Psychosis was my word losing to theirs. I abhorred and rejected them and felt mad whenever I overheard their discussions of my various indicators, worried as they were about my mercurial swirls from tearful melancholy to cheerful grandiosity. Meanwhile my visceral imagination invented the sick, magic world that was mine alone.

This illusory presence chased me down when I was very young. In the spring of 1993, my thoughts first spiraled into a gyre until I was the falconer. I was, at the time, sitting atop one hill of the National Park. I sat beneath the base of two trees grown together into a wooden V. In my madness I heard God tell me I was his second begotten son. It had rained that April morning, and what droplets remained glistened on the leafy floor of the forest. The brilliance of the noon-high soon lit a footpath for my lotus legs that felt as though it could lift me into the clouds. I could walk this way past the land, over the waves, to where water met sky. I was at the triple point, where all three phases can and do exist at once. Living water as ice, liquid, vapor: the trinity came to me, its voices sounding as clear as the squeak of a cellular phone. A brown cardinal landed on my shoulder, its hollow-boned weight like an incidental insect, only wider, spreading across most of my collarbone. A real vision in the reflections across water dark beneath the mist. A fire melted, and then boiled me, until I was as a cloud, gas clinging to dust. Her wingtips brushed my cheek as she flew away.

To return from the V tree, I had to climb a hundred-foot dune, descend a forty-foot valley, and then climb another hundred feet down the ridge overlooking my home. From the dune I could still see the old place. Its foundation was stone and the rest was red brick. Meant to rise above its neighbors, it was the largest structure on the broadest plot, atop a short dune so that its third-story attic overlooked even the yard's treetops. The place was set back among two acres of beech and maple forest at the end of Cherry Orchard Lane. Through these trees, the clearing of a wide back lawn dropped off a sheer seventy feet to the beach and its grass and then its sand and then its wetness before the horizon of fresh water, Lake Michigan.

Old trees made a shuffling ceiling of green above the path back to this home. When it comes to me now, where I am confined, just the memory of these woods gives me peace. I was full of religious ecstasy that first time, before I knew that faith and madness could be conflated until believing was reason enough for me to be locked up. I was bottling myself and corking that empty vessel. Everything was coming together and I had yet to be forced into feeling that such a feeling really meant that I was falling apart.

The first song I ever finished still resounds in my mind when I think of that unholy day:

> Innocence known in its absence,
> Nostalgia for the recent past -
> Omniscience of adolescence
> Cannot know how briefly it will last

I wish I could walk back there now and convince the boy I was that the unholy wraith who did in fact appear then was only myself. Only to the extent that I gave him power did he overpower me.

Dry World

I had journeyed half the way when a man straying from any path appeared on the highest ridge and descended, a man who appeared faint because of the unlikelihood of his presence just there and just then. He stood alone in that wilderness. Jesus Christ, I thought. The man was tall. He wore shiny loafers and a tailored suit, with a bandana cocked to the right where a tie should have been. Each item was the exact same shade of gray. His walking stick was black, with a knob atop it in the shape of a three-headed greyhound.

He appeared to be in his forties, but as the forest's light shifted, he was ten years older and then ten years younger. He wore the long, wide mustache that made him seem like an actor playing a police officer in one of those movies where the cops are far too stylish. Yet that resemblance ended with his countenance. The smirking twist to his smooth mouth brought to mind a self-satisfied, avaricious criminal who'd just opened a difficult safe.

"Jesus Christ," I said, if only to see if this figure would respond.

A hungry smile showed a single silvery crown around his upper left incisor, and this crown kept catching pieces of the sun and throwing them at my eyes. His hair was pepper salted with gray, and his eyes were an impossibly dark blue with stabs of gold radiating out of the pupils. He was close enough now for me to see as much.

"Excuse me, please." He had no discernible accent, but pronounced every consonant like an actor in the middle of an enunciation exercise. "I believe I have something of yours. But my news is terrible. You might need a drink beforehand. Some bourbon perhaps?"

"I'm thirteen."

"All the more reason, teenager."

"Hallucinations can't get you drunk."

"Yes, but they can kill. I'll show you now." He wiped the sweat from the back of his neck. On the back of my neck I felt my hairs stand. "Put out your hands." I didn't want to obey. Even more hairs were standing.

Jesus Christ, I thought. And, drawn as if by a string attached to his fingers, my palms outstretched, and he dropped the corpse of a brown cardinal, perhaps the brown cardinal. I clutched the bird to protect her from him. She was slight, cold and stiff, and her feathers poked through a gap in my trembling fingers.

"My cat," he said, "if you're curious who killed it."

I pushed him aside. His body was the opposite of the bird's: heavy as an x-ray blanket. Creepy density. I was sure he could see through lead and me. "Choose a life worth writing about or a life that's happy. Just know that it's one or the other. A snake eating snake. Serpentine choice, yours."

"I'm just writing..." I began.

Dry World

He cut me off, taking the fragment out of context. "You've chosen, then. Good to have someone who can empathize with me. You may yet be God." He took a swig from his flask, poured a splash on the ground and turned to leave. Then, over his shoulder: "If you're blessed, she's all I'll take."

"Who is she? I thought we were talking about God. What did I choose?"

I got nothing more. I only watched him, mesmerized by the pendulums of his gray legs, until he fell out of view behind the high ridge beyond the valley. When he was gone, I groaned as if I'd put down a prideful boulder and could rest at last. Then I went to find the V tree, old bird feathering my fingers. Its warmth grew slowly as I neared the place of peace. We reached my perch, and the spirit cheeped, and I could believe that the cardinal lived. My fingers spread in sync with its wings, flashes of flesh and brown and red, and there, on my tree, it landed on the elbow of the V. My eyes met its gaze and found that uniquely avian emptiness therein. When it had flown, I felt my mind fray like a branching fractal, complicating complexity, endless endlessness, and at last I knew how mad of a boy I was.

The doctors called it a break, all while assuring me that I wasn't broken. A psychotic break, they said. Mine was the rare madness come only from within. I'd never had a drug or a drink in my life, and there I was, thirteen years old and bat-shit crazy. There was no separation between my madness and me, no ironic distance. Not that first time. Every cell in my brain screamed in unison that I was God in the flesh come to save mankind from itself. I was still foolish enough to believe in myself then.

Dylan James Brock

The fever took months to break. My delusions had offshoots. Among my superpowers: the ability to know precisely to the second when a person was about to arrive some minutes before they did; direct contact with God, Mary, and the Devil, and the ability to tell within a second of meeting someone whether or not they had accepted Christ as their personal savior. Every sickness comes from somewhere, but that pat line about chemical imbalances in the brain didn't do enough to explain where I'd gone when I came back.

And I did come back. I responded to medication rapidly and ended up on a cocktail that kept me from getting too drunk on myself. Something like the shame I would later know in hangovers brought me low in the months that followed. Months gone, darkness when I usurped God through creation of my own. I may not have been broken buy my faith was. If my spiritual experiences could be wiped clean away by the right sort of pharmaceutical sanitation, what were the prophets but mentally plagued before proper mental hygiene was available?

Atheism and hedonism. I wore out both garments. With everything permitted, I allowed myself drunk after drunk and high after drunk and high. From the first drink in a glowingly starred disco in the Netherlands until that last drink I took at a wedding in 2003. Hunched by the last hangover, I coughed into a vomit stained pillow and then got up to get clean. I'd consumed as much as I could as quickly as I could.

So imagine my fury when told that only a spiritual awakening could cure me from the fallout of my spiritual awakening. Still, one of the twelve steps, the first to mention a higher power, promises that that higher power can restore one to sanity. That above all else I sought. A gentle bastard with some three decades sober told me that Alcoholics Anonymous was the only treatment he'd ever found that shut off the noise in his head. I wanted that peace but didn't want God. I got neither. Instead I wandered the limbo for those who behave well without belief. Before the death, the longest I put together was about a year. I have never seen the light without getting burned. Leave me in the darkness that I might rest.

Read this Rosetta stone carefully, for only in the passions we share will you decode the passions we don't. These are the glyphs of my private language waiting to be read by a twin. Before Narcissus can love a wood nymph, he must fall out of love with his identical sister. Try to see my reflection in this surf.

Chapter 2

Rain Froze Over Naked Limbs

Michigan

As of the day I left Ann Arbor in April of 2003, I had been there six years and was sick to death of the place. Just as I was going mad from the intolerable pretentiousness therein, arrogant intellectualism that reminded me too much of myself, filling my mind with florid voice-over, when I had begun the decent in the hell of a desert planet – only then did I meet the kind of woman for whom I'd searched since birth.

When her phone call came she was far from my fraying mind. I'd already rang my brother Paul to come and get me. I was so far gone I didn't even bother to open the windows as I chained cigarette to cigarette. Forget about stepping onto the balcony for a smoke. I was afraid that I might fall, terrified that I might jump. In this throat grip of suicidal insanity, I answered the phone.

"Hey, Gisele," I said.

"Hey, John. How did you know it was me?"

"I recognized your number. I got it from a friend."

"I got your number from a friend, too."

Dry World

"I was going to call, but I'm kind of in the middle of something. I really want to jump off a building, so I'm going home to Roosevelt to get better."

I was one misstep from death, but the part of me that didn't want to die wanted to live forever. I was laughing until I pissed myself: disgusting elation. The hospital felt inevitable unless the National Park could become a private ward.

"You're going home? You can't. You're going to write your book."

"I'll do it there," I said. I was high, she couldn't know, and low, too, not from drugs, but from taking no drugs at all. I was off my meds. I had not slept nor eaten in three days; I was spiraling, a dopamine cycle as empty as the wind.

"You can't move, John. We... you can't. I want to edit it. We need to be close and we can't be close if you're far so you can't move home. Can't!" She was mad as well. We'd only met the night before.

"Can't!!!" she screamed. She could not imagine how I heard her. "Can't." It split into a chord, harmonies shifted, every molecule between my ears sang, and there was another melody to write. The voices were beginning to direct me. Orders to write songs. Orders to take a black swan dive into a splatter of red and gray. My disease felt too pushy to be a mere cycle.

"Can't," she whispered.

But all I said was: "Hey, I have to go, have to write a song, have to pack, have to move."

"Do you need help? I can come over..."

And so, in the middle of a deathly fear scored by dissonant chords, I got hard. Know that the medications designed to keep the devil's visits infrequent also made getting hard at all remarkable. Why did this have to happen to me on such a day? Why did she have to have a man?

I met her just thirty-two hours before. Like me, Gisele was from a violent nest of WASPs, but in her case it was her mother who hit and berated her. Even now, years later, she remains the only woman who loved me as I loved her: creatively, obsessively, destructively.

"What's going to happen to your room?" Gisele asked.

My room? I could barely think about my room. Outside was that tiny balcony, the roof over a bay window on the second floor. The night before there had been another ice storm, and its crystals encased the tree limbs just beyond my panes. Orange streetlight reflected off their delicate lines, rendering wood into glass. Beyond was an apartment complex whose darkness cloaked dozens of sleeping undergraduates. No one would see me were I to follow orders and set the blowing fan aside and climb onto the ledge.

"I don't know," I said. "Someone else will move in."

Dry World

"I'll move in." I did not answer. I wanted a cigarette and fresh air. Breathing and nicotine made me calmer, even going so far as the hush the voices. I have since seen doubled-blinded studies that substantiate what had only been an intuition then. Cigarettes kept me sane, or at least more so. Without one, I was looking at the balcony and wondering if I dared.

"This will be perfect," she said. "I've always wanted to live in O' Neil. Leave as much as you want behind. Just take what you need."

"I wrote a song about you, Gisele."

"You didn't." Oh, that voice – my favorite song made husky by AM reception.

"I wrote it this morning. I still haven't slept."

"I can't stop thinking about your hands. Ever since we touched and mine seemed so small... I have to see you before you go."

It was six o' clock in the morning. The sallow sky above the adjacent apartment was fading the stars. I hadn't slept or eaten in three days. From my perspective she wasn't insane. She was just understanding.

"I'll be over in ten minutes. And I want to hear the song."

"I have to finish packing."

"I told you to leave it all behind. I'll take care of your things. I'm going to move in this afternoon. Tom will help me."

"Your boyfriend will help you move into some other guy's house?"

"I'll be over in five minutes."

Of course my brother would arrive soon as well, but I forgot that for the moment. I was gong to get laid. I knew it. In three minutes she was there. She didn't even knock. She opened my door, and just the sight of her in the wooden frame aroused a tightening of my trousers. She shed her jacket slowly, arching her back to tighten the fabric between her shelf-like breasts. The mad lady was my age, twenty-two. She had endogenously powdered skin, cell-bar lashes, and pleasing, symmetrical features best likened to a sexy goldfish.

"How did you get in?" I asked.

She did not answer. I met her gaze with a smile. She smiled back, slight spaces between her teeth, but a quizzical flicker of her nose was all it took for her to take me. I crossed the room, stepping over boxes with wide strides of my long legs. We embraced, tight, shelves pressed across my chest. I could have had her. She was mine. Instead I picked up the guitar, and she sat in the brown recliner by the door. I perched on the bed and began to pick out the memory of her song. I played my description of our only prior time together, this:

Dry World

On the way out I saw a picture
Of Halloween and her boy with her
And my blood it became a mixture
With the ice on the porch fixtures
So we swapped our parting words for smiles
And I hugged her for a little while
Then I left to walk the half a mile
Home on roads that were as smooth as tile

She said it was a great song, but that was all I got out of her. Paul arrived before we even got as a far as breakfast. He did not knock either.

Paul: blond where I was brown, brawny where I was scrawny, flannel where I wore a blazer, but the same eyes, the same nose, the same mouth. He slammed open the door with such force that both prints of dot-matrix fighters dropped from the loose tacks on which they hung.

"This is Paul," I said.

My brother glanced at startled Gisele but did not seem to think about what she might mean to me. As for Gisele, she soon turned her back on him, going through my boxes and unpacking what she wanted left behind. I watched the curves of her sweater, the arc of her jeans, her shifting presence, and drank her wafting fragrance.

"Bro," my brother said, "we need to drive now."

I was in love. I had no car. How could he not see? "Gisele just got here," I said.

"Fuck all that. I'm in the spot after you're drunk but before you're hungover and it's a small window, man. You know this."

"Give me an hour."

"Give me a cigarette. I'll be back when it's done." This time it was I who jumped at the slamming door. I was in love. I was insane. Why must these two go together like garlic and onion?

"Leave everything you can," Gisele ordered. "I'll keep you place for you. Where's the feather duster?"

Of course I didn't have one, but I couldn't concentrate long enough to tell her as much. All I could think about was that for which we hadn't the time: tearing my virginity into confetti and letting it shower out of the third story window, borne forward by a zephyr. I was that romantic. I was wholly a fool.

"One," she whispered.

"What did that mean?" I sat with my guitar and figured out the melody I'd hallucinated on the phone. She caught my gaze, shook her head, and then looked back to the shelves she dusted.

"One," she whispered again. This time I didn't ask, I just started bringing my things down. With a heavy bag I wanted to punch, I got to the porch. Now alone, I heard her again as I was setting down my bags – "one" – and I knew all three were only inside me. When I got back up to the room, she was on my bed crying. I sat next to her, but we didn't touch. I wouldn't do anything while she had Tom. Let him comfort her. She was his, after all. "Promise, John. Promise we'll get breakfast soon."

Paul kicked the door open. Gisele jumped and then wiped her tears. I rolled my eyes at Paul, but he did care about my romantic life just then. There were more important matters to him, I suppose – perhaps he could only see his weak, damaged brother going mad. He went back and forth carrying what was Gisele let us take down to his Jeep.

When he departed with the last of it, Gisele sobbed through wet gasps like a pet fish in hand, drowning in air through its cold gills. Her tears could have filled a glass bowl. I wrapped my arms around her sixty-nine inches of curving wire and lifted her light frame off the hardwood, picking her up and setting her down after half a spin. She shadowed me the whole way to the car, untouched. Look in the frame of Paul's rear view mirror: Gisele, crying under iced trees, glass branches glistening in the cold rising sun, as she foreshortens into a palpitating point and vanishes.

Chapter 3

All the Young Are Broken

New York

In May of 2005 I had been in New York City for eleven months. I was leaving a Friday night AA meeting, following my friend Sylvia downstairs and then through a foyer as thin as a hallway. There was a gilt pen lying on the floor. I pocketed it. There was my cell phone, which I took out and turned on. She struck me through the plate glass door before I got to the street, where, without warning, a white lake breaker crashed over the shallow shore of my heart's eye. On the lip of the curb, through a barrier of friends, there she stood – half-laughing, smiling, rocking like a metronome on her feet – my dead Michigan love, a blood rush lifting my feet three inches off the First Avenue sidewalk.

It was not Gisele. It was Gisele. The same oversized, wide-set eyes, the same fleshy, wide lips, the same upturned comma of a nose, twitching as my first love's had twitched, bewitching. With joy and wonder I saw again the peachy rim of abdomen between shirt and slacks where my Brooklyn bound mouth had nestled, and those nubile hips on which I had left the pallid prints of my hands while counterbalancing thrusts. Oh, that last implosive wedding night beneath sweaty bedsheets of Michigan air. Now in New York, she had materialized, and in the moment following this recognition, my whole twenty-four years fused into a chain reaction with every particle around, until the conflagration spread from me to the earth to the sun to the galaxy and beyond, and for an instant, the universe expanded more quickly.

Dry World

She was exactly the same on the downtown street. I was a tall, tottering, winsome stalk of junkie-thin waif-hood, an addict faced with his second hit of a drug whose first intake all but killed him. Yet I wanted more. The high, the fucking high I knew again at last, madness and love, was as indistinguishable as the woman who'd died and the woman before me.

"That is Billie," Sylvia said, her usually gypsum-soft eyes becoming diamond-hard.

"Has anyone seen a gold pen?" Billie arched her ostrich neck to shout over the crowd. That face: mild and wild at once, as if she might hold me in her arms for hours, only to bite my throat in the middle of a dream. It was the face that placed her inside my heart, careening from chamber to chamber. I produced my findings. Absently she took the pen from me, not bothering to let the exchange introduce us.

Billie wore birth-control glasses – they were that intentionally repulsive to men and popular with women at once. Even then I knew she didn't need those generic safety glasses. Her eyes were perfect. Metallic blue stabs in the dark. I wouldn't see the gold in them until it was too late.

All I could think was that I had to go to Sylvia's dinner, and that I would sit right across from her. I have great restaurant skills. They come from frequent dinners after frequent meetings. I position myself next to desired people no matter what. There was no choice but for Billie to take the empty chair across from me. Did she speak? She tossed word salad poems from memory within seconds of introducing herself. She was no dumb mute; she was a muse, and I could hers. We would be as ebullient as sugary soda's carbonation, and the bubbling was inside my brain like an aneurysm.

We talked about the program first. That's what one recovering alcoholic does when first meeting another. She was twenty-one, I was twenty-four, but I soon discovered I had been abstinent about a year longer than she had. A concise history of us: I had stayed sober since my first meeting, in Michigan, just after my brother Paul got married. She came into AA at eighteen, but Billie hadn't taken to the program her first go around. After a few relapses, she had put together nine months, three shy of being dateable. According to unwritten dogma of the program, one isn't supposed to date during recovery's first year. This is perhaps the most often broken rule in AA. It is such a joke that a fake step has been added to the program in jest, the thirteenth one. Really it belongs among the twelve traditions that keep sober people together for better or worse.

She pulled at her hair, as if about to tie its blackness into a ponytail, and exposed the fur under her lithe, long arms. Gisele, and the almost-girlfriend preceding her had both groomed themselves organically. We ate Indian food and sang "Happy Birthday" for Sylvia. When I went out for a cigarette, Billie said she wanted to join me. She asked for a light and cupped lithe, long fingers over my flicking hand. I felt such a spark I thought her Pall Mall Light might ignite before I ever flicked the flint. For the first time I couldn't precisely picture Gisele in my mind; already Billie was there instead.

Dry World

On the Sixth Street sidewalk I learned that we were both avid readers, so I asked what her three favorite books were – my same three in the same order. We had both lived in a commune for three years, though hers was a rural farm and mine was an urban boarding house. Both our high rents were paid by generous parents, and we were both ashamed of our dependence. We did work for spending money. We had only to make enough for cigarettes, coffee, food, and so she worked at a thrift store near her apartment on the Upper West Side and I worked at a Starbucks near my apartment in Little Italy.

I had another job, unpaid though it was. I was a research slave to the cryptic whims of that great American novelist Roger Abbey. He would send me deep into one library or another in search of documents on the history of parricide. I knew more about killing parents than any lunatic should know. Abbey was writing a nonfiction novel about a teenage madman who killed his entire family. I was there in part to give him the perspective of his killer.

"How did you get that job?" Billie asked.

"I'm from the town he's researching for his new book."

"I want to punch you in the face for being so lucky." Playful and deadly – who can resist such risky fun? Not an addict like me. I was already recalling the bloody taste of Gisele's attack: my ring, my nose.

I pinched my thick lower lip between my thumb and forefinger and thought of Gisele. I'm not dashing, but I look good enough to approach a beauty like Billie and be worth considering.

The scowl doesn't help my cause, but the night I met Billie, you couldn't smack the wolfish grin off my face. I just kept baring my fang-like eyeteeth. I had worn eyeglasses for nearly twenty years, so long that my face had grown of memory of spectacles lasers would never correct. But forget all that. She would love me before the night was done.

Billie stood only a few inches shy of my six feet. Legs made up half of her stature, and from the way her shallow denim swallowed her limbs, I knew her to be willowy. In bright urban night, her lines shone, highlights of her chest's gibbous ascent and abdomen's crescent descent. Meeting my eyes, Billie saw what I was noticing and pulled her vest together with a shiver. The streetlight haloed her auburn hair, but red streaks flanked her bangs like the horns of a cheap devil costume, only inverted. Something brought my hands to touch her hair.

My fingers wobbled like the tone of a tremolo pedal, medication shakes, as I stroke and said, "Vermillion."

"I distrust adjectives. They are as purple as an overstated simile."

"Suddenly I realize that you are versed in florid speech."

"Why have we yet to meet?" she asked me. She took my arm, and we interlocked like Legos. She shivered again, as if to let me know she touched me for warmth, but there was such assurance in her immediate trust of me. "You must know I hate Young People's meetings and young people. You're lucky you're so old. No, I hide out on the Upper West Side, or was trying to, until Sylvia dragged me down here."

"I love Sylvia. Somehow she's like your mom and one of the guys at the same time. Only as old as me and already the wisest woman I know." While we were speaking, I could smell the tea-tree oil on her, organic soaps that brought me back to my college commune in Ann Arbor, and brought me back to Gisele yet again. A passing vagrant mistook us for a couple and I paid him well for his words. Billie didn't bother to correct him, to my joy. I might have carried her to the top of Empire State Building had not the second suitor hit the stage, my boy Brian.

The beast joined us. Dreadlocks, red tips, black roots, nine facial piercing and sleeved tattoos: inked flesh ripped back to expose an illusory robotic exoskeleton underneath. This monster was wearing what he always wore, the sweater with a black image of the suffering Christ. Under that, his oft flashed badge, the orange T-shirt shot through with Taser burns. Brian the terrible was in my charge. I was his sponsor. And now he was clunking onto the pavement, burping in our faces. Six foot six in spiked platform boots. A grin so wide that the three shafts of metal through his tongue caught light.

"Brian, this is Billie."

"I know but did you know she's my fiancé?"

Billie twitched her nose.

"Yeah," Brian said, "we talk about how many kids we're going to have and what tattoos we going to give them ourselves." Billie's other arm was around Brian now and stroking his back with tensely curled fingers, as if she thought he needed a good scratch. She, like Gisele, was tactile and flirty by default, unless she made a conscious effort not to be. I wondered, for the first of many times, whether I might be just another one of the men who seemed to fall for her instantly, and whose love she maintained with every tease. Her hands on both of us, Brian and I eyed each other with something less than love for the first time ever.

"Billie Jean is her full name," he said, as if more knowledge about her was ice worth flossing. Please go away, I thought, although it was my responsibility to hang out with him.

He burped again and grinned again. Brian was not doing as much work on himself as I would have liked. Though still a year away from graduating high school, he had already gone a year without drinks and drugs, but he needed a great deal of attention. Now he was moon walking into passing pedestrians. His studded leather jacked billowed like a skirt while he spun on one foot, and a faux-robot hand grabbed his crotch. "Ow!"

"I'm his sponsor," I said.

"Billie loves the smell of my BO. And my burps, too."

Billie bobbed her narrow eyebrows but I couldn't tell if she were affirming or denying – she was that coy. Billie seemed to admire my patience with Brian. At meetings, Brian shared about hacking random faces with meet cleavers to get advice on how to make amends for the horrendous crimes he may or may not have done. I seemed to be the only one in New York City AA who was tolerant enough to sponsor the notorious Brian the Cleaver, as he was nervously known.

Brian still wanted more attention, so he pulled aside his sweater to reveal two circular holes in his T. "These are from the Taser," he told Billie. "I wear this shirt all the time to remind myself." Alcoholics love a low bottom story.

Billie took out a second cigarette and I followed her lead.

"I swung at my dad with a butter knife." He tittered.

Billie looked away from both of us and broke contact and stepped away. Madness seemed to bother her in a way that alcoholic insanity did not.

"So my mom locked herself in the bathroom with a cordless phone until the cops came and dad ran off into I don't know were. Then I got high until zap!" Brian faked a seizure, burning my overcoat with his cigarette. "They got me. I mean, jail, institution, rehab, and now fucking high school." He paused and sneered at me under smiling eyes. "Not like John. John was crazy enough to volunteer for a psych ward. What a good dog." He patted my brown curls as if I were a dying Chesapeake Retriever.

"My mom called the cops on me," Billie said. "I was only eating through my nose and I thought I was supposed to marry the messiah."

"My mom called the cops on me. I wanted a bunch of money to start a religion."

"I ran, boys, I ran away to libertarian commune."

"I went to the hospital for a month," I said.

"A month is nothing," Brian said.

"What religion was the money for?" Billie asked.

"Mine. I thought I was the messiah," I said.

Billie looked deeply into my eyes, so deeply and at such a short distance that I was sure she could see her reflection within them. After a pause, she swatted my head.

"Don't mock me, John."

"I am so serious it's funny," I said.

"That reminds me of a joke," Brian said.

I put a hand over my face but Billie pulled it away. We interlaced fingers and then broke apart, smiling though her eyes were terrified. Brian was scaring me more than he ever had. Every time Billie and I touched, he would wince as if we had both hit him at the same time. Yet he managed to tell his joke through the ticks of his faces.

Dry World

"This guy's doing a sexual inventory." Wince. "To his sponsor, the guy's like, 'There's something I didn't put on here. Something bad... I... I... I fucked a chicken.' And the sponsor is like, 'Oh yeah? Did yours die, too?"

Billie laughed far harder than I did. She even broke contact to hug him.

"No, I'm serious about that joke," I said. "It identifies identification. The only reason recovery works is because we're all chicken fuckers in one way or another. And at last, at last, it's like we found our birds of a feather."

"I don't know why I know what you mean but I know what you mean," Billie said. A serene silence, as silent as a downtown street gets. The rise and fall of her side returned to its place under my arm. Her head on my shoulder, leaning, and tea-tree oil rising from it as if it were violets resurrecting the season through the snowfall. We finished our cigarettes in a mellow spell I never wanted to end. Only after they were gone, and we had no reason to be out there anymore was there even a twinge of discomfort. Comma twitch of Billie's nose, quick tick of Brian's eyes, and then, I said, "We should get back in and pay."

We went inside. Inside twenty-one young alcoholics were mulling over the check looking pissed and betrayed because yet again we had all gone out to dinner at an endless table and now the check was short. Randy was describing eternity to a bored clique of girls. A thickening model was pointing out potential shots to Opal, who was snapping pictures with a manual Nikon. Sylvia just stared at the check as if she could set it on fire with her eyes and make our responsibility disappear. Billie and I had to throw down an extra five each. The group exited as a herd. Outside twenty-one young alcoholics crowded the sidewalk looking bored and bothered.

There Billie and I stood side by side, her right hand slapping my left. Reach, slap. Reach, slap.

"Stop, John, stop," Sylvia said as if we had everything to do with her.

"Stop what?" I asked.

She didn't even bother answering. It was assumed that I would concede my love life was Sylvia's business. To let me know, she just shook heard head and smirked.

"All right. What are we doing?" Sylvia asked. "Karaoke or Hookah?"

"I love how there's not another choice," Billie said.

"Billie Jean Schlegel," Sylvia said as a mother might say a name and only a name to guilt the child more than any shout could. I went for Billie's palm and for the first time, her slap stung.

"John." Now it was my turn to be chastised. I was making too hard a play for the new girl.

"For someone so quick to pass judgment you sure are slow making up your mind," I said.

"Fuck you! It's my birthday," Sylvia said. "Ok. Half the kids can't get in the bar. So Hookah. Ok. Hookah."

Sylvia was my closest girl friend, sober ten years at twenty-four and den mother to us baby alcoholics. She had the wide hips of a Jewish Mother of twelve, and to us, she was one. I had gone without a psychologist since my move to city, and Sylvia acted as my therapist. Her insights were as incisive and surprising as my best shrink's had been. Through her apple-scented hair, I whispered, "How come I haven't met Billie before?"

Her eyes became a boomerang I had thrown with my question – they got distant, very distant, and then hooked around and came straight at me, ready to strike. "She hasn't done a sexual inventory," Sylvia whispered. The sexual inventory. A confessional diary that you would never want anyone to read, that would make your mother blush. The purpose of this document was to see the pattern of love and sex in all its gory details, to show your sponsor in hopes that you had half a shot at a "healthy" relationship with members of the opposite sex.

"I can hear you both," Billie whispered, stepping ahead, walking backwards in front of us. "Sylvia keeps her friends safe from crusty old predators like you, John." Billie's eyes were like a wounded fawn before a grizzly, acquiescing to the inevitable. Fate allaying fear. The clomps of approaching platform boots. The spikes on them so long I could almost hear what was on top of the shoes. Brian took Sylvia's arm and he discussed his inevitable marriage to Billie. I didn't know whether he was mocking me or making his case, but for the moment, I didn't care. His move had left me alone with my new one. Fawn look from Billie. I stroked her hair.

Billie punched me in the stomach, punched me hard, punched the wind out of me. Sylvia held her eyes shut and shook her head so she did not see me accelerate to catch Billie. God knows what she must have thought of me when she opened them and there I was with an arm around the woman who had just doubled me over.

There was only half an endless avenue block to go and I had to make it happen. Billie had to love me before we got there. So I did what I do better than talking, I sang, knowing it to be ridiculous, I sang, knowing it would make a scene, I sang this:

> In the center of New York
> The women are un-win-able
> This place made them too cynical
> To fall for a blue dork
> In the center of New York
> Where the whole world is spin-able
> And every bear has been a bull
> Broken by a screw job's torque
> In the center of New York

"Who wrote that?" Billie asked.

"I did." Her eyes squinted as if the fake glasses she wore were the wrong prescription.

"I've heard it before." Nose Twitch. "Is that Sylvia's profile song on MySpace?"

"It's mine."

"I have this feeling you think you're a genius and I'm starting to worry you might not be entirely wrong."

Dry World

"All my life I've been told as much."

"It doesn't count coming from your mother."

"Not just from her. From Roger Abbey, too."

Chapter 4

Nature Wasn't Nurtured

Michigan

Paul drove me home to Roosevelt with a road beer in hand. The whole state was covered in ice, and a cold sun cast a surreal shine over the encasement, as if the world were made to shatter. Everything was so delicate in my state, and I didn't yet know how to handle it. My mind was cycling into shreds, as if its neurons were a yarn ball chased and torn by a cat. I knew that cat's name, and knew no seat belt or straight jacket could keep me safe from him. My brother kept looking over at me, perhaps looking at my twitching eyes, though I couldn't know. I never looked back at him. I only saw his head turn in my peripheral vision. I could not take my eyes off the ice under a cold, cold sun, and the flashes of rainbows spraying through the prisms of the freeze.

Perhaps to break me out of my brain freeze, Paul slid in a cassette of my music and let it play. I looked at him at last and he smiled weakly. His eyes were flecked with red and pink but still shone with an unfrozen liveliness. Paul smiled weakly, and then gave me a stern nod, as if perhaps he wanted to pat my head but thought better of it now that were grown. He had always acted as my protector, as a sort of police force that abused its power but kept one safer than a department that played it straight ever could. I sensed that he wanted again to keep me secure from myself, sensed it in the way that brothers can know what each other are thinking through thorough familiarity. Yet we were men, or almost that, and so we left our intimate connection unspoken and he turned up the radio.

> Met myself on a long walk home
> We picked a fight promptly
> One of us died and one of us walked
> I no longer know which one was me
> As a child Ulysses was
> My mother's bedtime story
> Her cryptic words and my father's slurs
> Bespoke their feelings for me
> Father's gone to bed with his girlfriend
> Mother's work and troubles never end
> Nature wasn't nurtured properly
> When I fell from this twisted tree

When it finished, Paul smiled widely and said, "Christ, now I want to kill myself, too." He laughed and I laughed. We sometimes make light of wrist slitting and shotgun meals, Paul and I, if only because laughter is often the best way to cope with insanity.

"You know sometimes when I smoke too much pot I can't sleep because I'm sure you're going to kill yourself. My thoughts just go back to finding you dead over and over. I don't get paranoid about myself. I get paranoid about you, you fucking prick."

"Paranoia would imply that your fears are groundless. I am eighteen times more likely than the general population to die by my own hand. Your fear is entirely reasonable."

"You see, you bitch? It's shit like that that freaks me out. That kind of crap is why mom's been up all night crying so many times. Why dad freaks out and locks you up. You don't fucking get it man. You hurt us when you threaten yourself."

I said nothing. I only lit up a cigarette and popped out the tape before the song ended. Then I put in a cassette of icy pads washing over spacey guitars. A warbling baritone rose over the desolation like a winter bird, and I knew Paul knew why I chose that band. The lead singer had died by his own hand. I was lashing out by my implicit and explicit threats. I owed my family nothing. All they had ever done was love me in spite of my hateful, hurtful affliction. Without them I would have been dead years before. Forget about graduating from college as I was about to. I would have never lived through high school if my father hadn't thrown me into a bin until I was safe again. In the midst of a mental illness, the pain can be so great that the selfishness at its core becomes impossible to recognize. I was beyond that point. I knew my problems were hurting Paul and Mom and Dad and even George. Yet this self-awareness was a hopelessly insufficient against that very illness. So I smoked on, killing myself in smooth and mild installments, waiting for the cowardly courage to make the final push and end my suffering in a manner that brought suffering to everyone left behind.

Halfway to Roosevelt we stopped at a gas station so Paul could get a forty. I used the bathroom and found my ancient friend waiting for me at the urinal. The dark one still wore all gray, with that bandana cocked to the side and his crowns flashing the fluorescent light back at me through his hungry smile. I shook off the shivers and went for the stall next to him. He kept looking at me from an uncomfortable closeness. There were only two stalls. I was waiting for him to engage me as he did whenever my madness took over, but he seemed to be in quiet mood. He did look down at my crotch and laugh, a shaking brassy rumble that echoed against the hard surfaces. At last I took no more.

"Where are you going with all this?" I asked.

"You've met the one, I hear."

"You stay the fuck away from Gisele."

"I should give you the same advice, but you'd think me a liar."

"You can't speak truth if you try," I said.

"That doesn't mean much coming from someone delusional. You can't even differentiate the true from the false," he said, and laughed again.

"I'm not scared of you anymore. You'll be gone again as soon as they get my doses right. That bandana is a joke."

He flushed the toilet and walked over to the sink. With steady grace he washed his hands thoroughly, meticulously, and then looked at the available towel. It was one of those rolls of fabric that looks as if a washing is needed again after drying hands with it. The dark one shrugged and pulled off his bandana. After he wiped the water from his hands, he tied the damp cloth back around his neck.

The gray man sighed. "If only I could die like she will. Then maybe we'd both get some peace." And with that, the fear left me and I was able to leak at last. He winked a blue-gold eye at me and then swayed through the door without a sound.

When I got back in the car Paul had already twisted the top off of his beverage but was waiting until he was out of view to consume it. We slid back into traffic and he gulped down a swig of the malt liquor.

Annoyed, I decided to sleep off the strangeness. There is a place between waking and napping where mild hallucinations are entirely normal. I was there when I saw myself enter my safe place, the dry world.

I would go to a cold desert planet when I wanted to be safe from everything, when I wanted only the stars overhead to guide me. I was there, under a pink-tinged sky. The sun was smaller and barely of any use. Other stars could be seen in the heavens opposite it. The constellations were all gone, the patterns were entirely alien, and so I tried to fit them into pictures and make up my own myths about them. In the center of the sky there was perfect pentagram, a five-pointed star within a ring, each key dot a sun of its own. I looked away, disturbed by the devilishness of the symbol.

There is water on the dry world, but it is all frozen into sand coated glaciers. My throat was parched and there was nothing to quench it. I looked as I had in the car, dressed in a thrift store suit, unequipped for any sort of desert expedition. Only on the horizon did I see hope for slaking the thirst. There was a black clad figure, wrapped in tunic and a veil, looking like a Bedouin wife separated from her family. I ran toward her while she stood fast, and as she approached I could tell her body was beautiful by the way the wind wrapped the black fabric around her. When we were close, I saw the bluest gold eyes I had just left behind, the eyes of Gisele, and the eyes of Billie. From her tunic she produced an ivory knife, and when she wrapped my hands around its handle, there was heat in her touch, the heat of a desert on earth, strange and out of place in that desolate waste.

I awoke when the car decelerated enough to jolt me upright. We were at that first stoplight where I–96 ends in an expressway that divides the watered rich from the drier poor. The money in Roosevelt follows the shore, and to my left I could see the hill high houses above the rim of Agawatta Lake and to my right I could see the squat tenements of the poor who could only afford to view the rich. We were home, on the border of Roosevelt Shores and Roosevelt Heights, the suburban enclave and the urban blight. The light turned green and we headed deep into the dunes, up and over their paved rolls, toward the National Park that I hoped would keep me safe from the encroachment of evil developments.

Paul's forty was gone and rattling and clinking in the backseat as we hit the stop signs that gated the entry into our deepest of subdivisions. Just as we slipped down the last turn my phone rang. It was Gisele.

"I had that dream again," she said.

"The phone's going to cut out soon."

"What? I can't hear you. I had that dream about the desert and the devil." And at that, the call was lost and so was I.

My parents were absent. Paul grabbed a six pack of Heineken from the fridge and turned around right then to head back, apparently pleased that he had avoided them altogether.

Dylan James Brock

I found my dog and took her for a walk on the beach. As the lion hound bounded around me, I looked only at my feet, as if blinders could make the sand there stretch to the horizon, so that the beach was a planet where I'd find safety and love, but eventually I had to look up.

Chapter 5

Like a Burned Journal Page

New York

New York City's heavens were ruddy with the reflected life of those million lights who burn against night's dying. The clouds were spreading enough to split like the transient shadows of an eclipse. In the damp haze after the rain and before the moon, Billie shined. There on the patio behind the hookah bar, the remnants of the day's rain glistened in the night. Pools collected in the hollows of the plastic chairs, so we sat on their edges. Three-quarters of an inch separated my knee from her knee.

"One?" Billie asked, bound in suspense, as if wrapped in the confines of a corset.

"One," I answered. "One woman in twenty-four years. Pathetic, I know." My right hand rubbed my cheek and I wondered if I looked as palely powdered as I felt.

"Zero might be pathetic, John, but one, one is…" Billie sighed as if she could breathe free for the first time since morning.

Her jeans were tucked into tailored leather boots. The way they curved with her calves, tight to the thin lines, I appraised their value: a month's rent. "Where did you get those?" I asked, pointing.

"I won't tell. Everything else is from my thrift store."

"I think I'm infatuated with them."

I reclined into the water in my seat, coldness collecting around my backside. She took out the third cigarette since we'd come outside. I lit it and while her fingers cupped over mine, I took her hand in my hand. She stroked the back of it with her free palm. After her nose twitched, she smiled, and that nose bunched into wrinkles that rolled like young dunes. I'd first kissed Gisele on low rolling sand, and thought of kissing Billie then.

She gave me a last pat on the hand and reclined into her own puddle.

I needed another cigarette now, but the flint didn't take until Billie cupped her hands around the breeze. This time her touch was only incidental.

"Where are you?" Billie asked, her eyes white dwarfs, the starry night I sought.

"Michigan," I said. "Roosevelt. I've got to go home."

Billie squinted. Her glasses came off, opening the lines of her face. "I don't even need these. When I want to be someone else..." A gust, and the stray droplet from the umbrella above us blew onto my lens. I took off my glasses and saw Billie underwater; I was swimming with open eyes. She reached for my frames and cleaned them for me. "Don't go back to Michigan."

"Now home is Little Italy. I meant bed." Through my watery blur, I imagined she actually looked relieved. There was no way to say, though. She dropped her cigarette and ground it out with her pricey heels. I put on my glasses and surfaced.

"Do you have a roommate?" Billie asked.

Startled by where such a question could take us, I twitched. A gray shaft of ash collapsed onto my overcoat. She wiped it off.

"Two bedroom. Me and my little brother George." George, who was probably drunk and stinking up the place. I worried about a clash between lives: my home life, my sober life, and my love life. How would she react to facing active alcoholism? She was newly sober, but it was a risk I was willing to take with all requisite selfishness.

"I trust you, John. I don't know why but I have since the first time I saw you." Nose twitch. The smile was there, gentle corners bent on eyes and lips. I had to know her well to know it was genuine, and somehow, after only minutes, I did. She was going home with me.

We left through an alley, didn't even say goodbye to the gang. They would all be at an Upper East Side meeting the next night anyhow.

I walked slowly down the few blocks of Houston, stalling in hopes that George would leave. So often I made that crowded journey alone after nights out, but now I had radiant company. We moseyed in a night whose wind was warming into a breeze. The next day would be milder. Looking for a way to fill the wordless

vacuum, I reached for a device in my tight pocket. I split my
headphones, and we listened to one of my recordings, but I didn't
tell her whom she heard.

> I am gonna be a star
> And no matter where you are
> In the church of in the bar
> You'll hear me and my guitar

As we listened to the lowest string resonate, dropped as it
was a whole step and powering through the mix, I felt at once
removed and intimately connected, as if I were making a long
distance phone call to my lover. But Billie was here now and we
were nearing my place, and my little brother. I slowed my pace.

We turned down Elizabeth Street and the city softened like
the moon seen without my lenses. Young trees shuddered under
the shadows of the red tenements. I knew my brother's schedule
and it was this that made me dawdle past the crowds at closing
bistros and past the gated boutiques. The brick boxes broke into a
chain link square of grass and sculpture, a private garden even I
couldn't enter. The clouds were clearing quickly. Above the
buildings on Mott Street the moon hung like a sickle that had
reaped the sky of all its sparkles.

I stopped. My brother should have been leaving any
moment. I could have sent him a text and he would have left, but I
didn't. She was too much with me to break and contact anyone else.
She took the player from my hands and checked the artist. "Who is
John Rook?"

Dry World

"He's from Roosevelt Shores, Michigan, but he tells people Roosevelt to make it simpler."

Billie pushed me, a shove that yanked out her earbud. It dangled across the sidewalk, and I let it dangle. When she stooped to pick it up, I caught a flash of the downy chest beneath her loose brown sweater. She saw me see her. She blushed and pinched her blue vest with her left, and then feigned another punch with her right. I caught this delicate fist and held it, pausing there in the door frame. George, I thought, please don't be home.

"What's the wait?" Billie asked. I shrugged.

Before we reached the second floor I knew that George had not gone. We could hear him, screaming along with a riffing rock record.

Suddenly everything was wrong. I should have never asked Billie to come back here. Alcohol doesn't bother every recovering alcoholic, but I barely knew her. I couldn't know how she'd react to my partying brother. The smell of bourbon hit us when the metal door swung open with a clang. Billie didn't say a word, but her eyes were like sketches of eyes – flat, still.

In front of us stood my brother, a sturdy six feet of lumberjack musculature. His orange jeans hung over red hush puppies that stomped the polished hardwood in time with the blaring rock. In his left hand was a fifth of Old Grand Dad. His right hand strummed power chords over it as if the bottle were an electric guitar. So hard was he rocking out that he didn't notice us until his song ripped through to its end and he could hear us creaking across the old tenement floor.

George pivoted on one foot as the other began to stomp in time with the beat of the next rock song he'd lined up to play. His face could be seen through the strands of his brown mop. George looked like a portrait of me done by a flattering street artist: nose even where my nostrils differed, brow patrician where mine was simian.

George shouted greetings and good tidings as he turned down the computer speakers. The next song kicked in more softly. "What news?" George asked me. It was line he took from a biography of Mao. Apparently the dictator greeted his underlings thusly.

George and I had a mutual fascination with the ridiculousness of communism in practice. I gave him the usual response. "The revolution is perpetual, comrade, and we fight on in the name of the workers."

"How's NYU treating you?" Billie asked my brother. I hadn't told her where he went to school. George glared as a minority might at a profiling cop. He had been stereotyped. Now his eyes were flat and still sketches. They greeted each other and went through introductions. George kept staring straight through her, as if she were a translucent specter. I'm sure her resemblance to Gisele made the whole encounter spooky for him. He looked scared enough to flee and did as much.

Dry World

"I'm long John gone. God knows there's a party somewhere just waiting for these moves." George said, draining the last of the fifth with a gulp. The apartment smelled like a retiree drinking himself to death.

A red and black plaid davenport, a bear skin rug, and the mounted head of a buck my grandfather shot in the nineteen-sixties: the motif was that of a cabin in the north woods. Billie looked at once fascinated and disturbed by all the taxidermy. "Grandpa shot that the day Nixon was elected president."

"I feel like I'm relaxing at a lake retreat," Billie said. "It's a lot like my commune was."

George was bundling himself with a lime scarf and a teal cap. "Delicious meeting you," he said, shaking one of her hands with both of his. Billie flipped down the mitten flaps on George's fingerless gloves so that they would cover his tips and kept him warm. Then she patted his head and sent the guy on his way. George was almost out the door when he stopped himself. He pivoted again, this time running for the freezer. He got a bottle of Arrow Vodka out of the freezer, dropped the pint in his pocket, and skipped out the door. I slammed it behind my brother and most of the smell left with him. His hush puppies echoed down the stairwell in the silence he left behind.

When the door closed I turned to look at Billie and found her eyes still sketchy. I wanted to caress the inside of her elbows, perhaps even throw an arm around her shoulders and squeeze her gently, but something held my arms fast to my sides. I knew this was not okay. I had brought her to a wet face in a wet place and now she could tell that I wasn't living the healthy lifestyle. If I wasn't teetering on the edge of relapse, she might be after this alcohol-soaked encounter. She took a step back from me and asked for water.

I had to wash a glass for her. As the faucet hissed into the cleansing bubbles, I heard Billie singing a lullaby whose lyrics I couldn't make out and whose melody I couldn't identify.

My mother used to sit on my bed's foot and sing that one, never touching me until she said goodnight. That Billie knew the song at all was strange, but that she knew all its words felt inexplicably meaningful. When the glass was dry she pointed a gun-like finger at the deer and asked if my Grandfather was still alive.

"He died the day George was born in the same hospital and everything."

"How?"

"Liver. My family tree's lit up like Christmas."

"I noticed." When I asked her, Billie insisted she wasn't bothered by the booze. Yet it seemed as though she were lying to herself so that she could believe she was telling me the truth.

She took off her vest and dropped it on the bear rug's head. "Don't want him watching me sleep." She wrapped herself in a deer pelt blanket and stretched across the davenport. How serene she looked taking up any room I might have used to put moves on her. Her lids were down. Her lips were closed. I went to the closet and fetched my childhood blanket, green and white checkers of wool. I draped it over her and knew that I was feeling better and hoped that she felt likewise. It might even be okay after all.

When I opened the window to air out the alcoholic scent and switched on the fan, I felt no chill in the outside air. It was as if the whole world were warming around us to keep us comfortable in our time of need. I thought of George sweating through his scarf and cap and laughed to myself. For all his quirks, my brother kept our place tidy. I fetched Billie's empty glass of water and took it to the dishwasher. When I returned to the couch to curl in next to this girl I found her already asleep.

"Billie?"

I swear she smiled slightly, like a yawning cat. Her silence and stillness convinced me that she needed the rest and I let her stay there, her deep breaths purring with each heave of her chest.

"Night," I said but she was too deep in to do much more than fall in deeper.

I want to remember Billie now as she appeared then, the deepening amplitude of her gently pulsing chest.

Chapter 6

Out into the Deep

Michigan

On an April Friday Gisele came to visit Roosevelt. My parents were out of town and my little brother was babysitting me. I was a young twenty-two and George was an old sixteen. His job was to make sure I didn't end my life. This meant he got to miss a Friday of high school. As fun as all that might sound, George seemed resentful. His pretty eyes were weary, wary, aged. I barely acknowledged him.

I had to attend to my writing in the hopes that venting might keep me from imploding. When mad, I rarely notice the damage I do to those around me in the name of healing myself. Only after the mixed curse passes do I feel hung over from my dry benders.

I kept busy with my novel, and writing felt like melting ants with a magnifying glass. I had chosen a first person omniscient point of view so that I could be the God over those who had punished me. I wrote, I sang, I raged, against, my first girl, my Chloe, whom I had given the power to make myself into a suicidal virgin, whose inflictions would later seem like Indian burns, childish and playful compared to the charred blisters Gisele would leave me with. I hurt Chloe far worse than she hurt me. I assailed her with exaggerated slander and hyperbolic libel. If only I had kept it to myself, I might have healed without hurting her. Instead, I published and publicized the words as I wrote them, a sort of glorified live journal that felt like a new art form back then in 2003, before the global warming of a hot air explosion we now call the blogosphere. Hundreds saw the smoke signals of my ire. Gisele was only one of them, but she became an avid fan. So much did she enjoy the taste of my vitriol that she decided to pay homage and drove the miles to visit me.

What began with an idle offer to come my way became a reality that I never thought was really going to happen. She was calling me for directions to my parents' house. But first the inquiry as to my stability, and I still somehow hadn't figured out that it was my very madness to attracted her to me.

"Have you slept?" she asked through my phone.

"I saw the devil in the pale moonlight." I pumped my legs on a squeaking porch swing. The chain was singing a fourth above the auditory hallucination of an angel holding an alto pitch. "There was only his silly silhouette but I know it was him." I flicked my butt over the fence of the neighbor's yard. This porch was where I came for breaks from my desultory postings. I had been in the middle of a sentence comparing Chloe's refusal to perform fellatio to the first temptation of Christ – "man cannot live by head alone" – when the phone had rung and it was the new girl. She seemed intrigued by my descriptions of the dark character haunting me. "Who else wears a beret around here?"

When she said she'd see me tonight, I replied, "Make it to-afternoon," and hung up on her.

I returned to study and found a breeze had scattered a printout of my first posting around the room. Cold black coffee filled fractions of mugs dotting the surface of the desk, the shelves, and a sewing table. Scratched discs of upbeat songs gleamed from under many of these cold cups, whose coasters would keep getting damaged right until I slid them into the system and blared them, skips and all. At this moment the speakers were already pumping without my doing. George had made his own selection from my damaged favorites and was playing along on his acoustic guitar.

I told him Gisele was on her way to our house, and he smiled as if in bemused disbelief, seeming as he might have had I insisted on the existence of Santa Claus and he couldn't bear to break down my charming delusion. An instant into his smile the CD stuck and skipped, a microsecond sample. The stutter of the rock's flow seemed to fit the empty cycling of my thoughts.

Everything was where it was supposed to be. The stereo's clock read four minutes past two. I had only two sessions left before Gisele arrived. And so I wrote, but that's all I did. I plugged in my headphones and wrapped myself in music and tuned out from anything more than my turbulent emotions. I turned off my cell phone and unplugged the internet connection, so that the only distraction was our lion hound, who seemed to love the sound of my fingers clicking and did lay her heavy head in my lap, but would lift it as soon as I stopped typing. I didn't stop typing, though, not until an hour had passed and an album had run its course and it was time to break for a cigarette. The dog pawed at the screen door when I returned to the porch, pawed because it wanted to stand close to me and sniff the secondhand smoke. Every time she would wait until I lit up and then it was after me. I let the dog out and she closed on me and joined in on the puffing as usual.

The next hour passed likewise – ignored George, indulging animals – until I had written something like ten thousand words in a little less than eight hours. I was gloating over my scattershot prolificacy when I turned my phone on and three-seconds later Gisele called.

"I've never been lost in my life but I'm lost now, John. You can't know how good my sense of direction is. Where am I?"

She asked about a causeway that meant she had gone too far north and I directed her back toward me.

"What do you think it means that only I could get you lost?" I asked.

"I'm a mile away now. I can feel it." And I could hear her motor rev through the phone as the lion hound kept up its intoxicating sniffs. I put headphones back on but I still heard her car before I saw it, the whirr of its Swedish motor as the old, old Saab climbed our inclined driveway. My knees shook as I stepped toward, as if I had sea legs from months spent distant from any women. In reality it had only been a week since I had last seen Gisele and I was still corresponding with Chloe every day in one manner or another. My isolation from women was in most ways the sort of delusion that must be broken for my own well-being, as a child has to be reassured that there is no goblin beneath his bed. I was still adrift in a dervish of my own doing, but putting my arms around Gisele felt anchoring.

When I saw the pearls around her heron neck, I knew this occasion meant as much to her as it did to me. I positively shook when I embraced her. And she stroked my wobbly arms as I felt the front of her move me.

"I love the way you quake," she whispered. I kissed the top of her head, the strands sticking to my lips, tasting of tea-tree oil.

At this point George stepped out onto the porch, walking and reading. Still he managed to step – without looking away from his text – around the dog who sat between us brothers. When he glanced away from the pages, pleasant disbelief found him and raised his brow. Yes, there was a Gisele.

"That was my favorite book," she said, surprising me.

I notice George was reading my tattered paperback of Dune, scrawled annotations and all.

"I thought your favorite was To the Lighthouse," I said.

"Was. It was Dune at his age."

George introduced himself only after he buried his nose back in the novel, though he did shake her hand. He seemed to be intent on finding a meaningful place to stop, but when he did he looked up with grave authority. Summoning a sternness that reminded me of my father, only with a deeper voice, he spoke. "Gisele, John is not well. You know this?"

Dry World

"Suicide is the rational consequence of an irrational world. I think people who never want to end life themselves are the ones who aren't well."

"My parents gave me directions. I can't let him out of my sight for more than twenty minutes. He's going nowhere without me."

"Your parents didn't know I would relieve you of duty."

A silence stretched, taut, while my little brother considered the offer and seemed to consider the one offering it even longer. Perhaps he thought she made too minor of an objection to an act as destructive and selfish as suicide; perhaps he thought about how great her tits looked in that sweater; perhaps both. In time, he did smile, broadly and with those genuine twists to his eyes that are so hard to fake, and he seemed to understand that she was something I needed. "He's yours, now."

Two minutes later we were in the Saab, a mix tape blaring through its tinny speakers. I ejected the cassette. Her wide, thick lips curled into a frustrated sneer. I had violated her control of the car just when the beat of her songs seemed to flow like dashed lines beside tires. And I had done it to play her a recording I made of myself in my bedroom, a lengthy piece of me pining for Chloe:

> I consider kissing you
> But I know you have yet to
> Heal from the heart surgery
> Of your ex-lover's perjury
> Though you're all I want to get
> I tag you and say you're it
> Don't know if you feel the same

So we keep to our safe game
When we leave it I watch you dress
Looking inconspicuous
While I pull on my own clothes
And wonder where my courage goes
We join the beach fire and drink
And when I catch your eye I think
If I could give you my thoughts
I'd finally find what I've sought

She was pleased, but I didn't need to know if she liked the song. I needed to know if Gisele liked me as Chloe had never seemed to. I asked what her man thought of her coming to see me. When the answer didn't come immediately, I looked away from her, preparing myself for bad news. By then we were almost downtown, and arcing around the curves following the shore of Agawatta Lake, the Little Lake, the Harbor: it is known by all theses names. Only I knew what lay at the end of the boulevard, beyond the marquee lights of the Dover Theater, past the inscribed edifice of the Roosevelt Museum of Art, and further than the buttresses of the Dover Public Library's cathedral to books. There, past the sites, was nothingness, the rubble of a demolished city center, a hole in the heart of my home so devastated that it looked as though it had been bombed into pieces. As I waited still for her answer, to find out how it was going to be, I felt an emptiness at my core that I still was silly enough to believe the right woman would fill. And when at last she spoke, for a short while I did feel completed.

"I broke up with him to be with you, silly boy." Her nose twitched after she spoke. We were parked by then. I had guided Gisele into a spot across the street from the demolition's remains. To get to the ruins, we pulled down the orange mesh of a plastic fence and stepped over and around debris.

Dry World

Atop a pile of shattered cinder blocks pierced by a distended steel shaft, I took Gisele's hand in mine for the first time. To understand what this meant you have to know that, in my family, we barely ever touch each other. Even my own mother went only as far as the occasional pat on the shoulder. Touching Gisele at all, initiating that contact, felt at once intensely intimate and arousing. Our surroundings made this feeling of connectedness seem to isolate us from everyone else, and the apocalyptic scenery helped further this atomization. We stood alone as the only people left after a nuclear strike.

"What was this?" Gisele asked, her eyes burning.

"City planners thought they could save the downtown by putting a roof over it." She rubbed the back of my hand with her thumb and I thought I was about to implode and collapse. "The Roosevelt Mall went down six weeks ago."

"I have these recurring nightmares where I'm the only one in a wasteland where the world used to be. This is the apocalypse in my sleep. It looks just like this."

"I can make your dreams come true," I said. I squeezed her soft palm.

Gisele laughed like hydrogen, light than air and incendiary. She burned herself for me with every look of sympathy. There was a spark in her sparkles that threatened to inflame everything around her, and she spread it to me.

"I see the future when I get migraines," she said. "It comes in flashes. Light becomes colors. Colors become pictures. And the pictures see through me. I've seen this before and I thought it meant the end of the world, but it was only Roosevelt." Broad eyes disturbed as rubble still falling in the midst of a collapse, destroyed and settling into their destruction. "But the future never goes past this summer. These flashes of now – I thought they meant we would all die somehow. After this, I don't think so. I think only I will be dead before September. And I know how now." Closer, at her irises: the translucent skein of cirrus foretelling a coming storm. Their aspect of despair before fate burned through the heart of my head.

Gisele squeezed my hand hard and when that wasn't enough, she twitched her nose. I patted her soft hair. She didn't have to his through blood that I come with her to the suicide forest. I thought I knew that I was going there too. Here was the reason that Gisele left a stable man for a suicidal child. She understood me all too well, and now I understood her, too.

"If you would tear a little twig from any of these plants, the thoughts you have will also be cut off," I cited.

"Let's go find your tree. The V tree," she said. And we held hands all the way back to her Saab, until I couldn't tell whether my hands shook or her hands shook because we shook together, holding such terrified excitement.

She drove, a scenic route, down Lakeshore and the long way around to Beach Street. Just past the plaque where Buster Keaton once lived, the foliage parted above the pavement and a mauve sky spread, framing a sinking vermillion disk. As the light bled across the silhouettes of pleasure sloops, not one motorboat whirred to disturb the postcard painting. Gisele pulled her auto to the side of the road, and I could feel a moment of discovery coming.

"We'll have to find the tree in the morning," I said, pointing my bent finger eastward, at the blackening woods flanking the shoreline. She switched off the car and we stepped into the brisk twilight. Noticing the chill in the air, she opened her trunk and removed a green-checkered blanket. "That was my first," I said.

"That's why washed it. Still stinks like you, though," she said, and then draped it over herself like a shawl, still touching the corners where the wool folded at her shoulders.

I didn't need to see the future in migraines to know then that falling for Gisele was embracing an enemy with a dagger in his hand. I would be betrayed but enjoy the dangerous intimacy in the meantime. We stepped over a short steel rail and the sand gave under my feet, spilling in around the corners of my brown loafers. West Michigan sand is almost entirely pure, ground Quartz. I dropped my old corduroy blazer on sand that she might sit above the soft grains. Her denim skirt slid high on her thighs, red from the ankle length tights underneath, and I had no idea what to do with this woman, though she had plenty of ideas for both of us.

I rubbed my right eye and lost a contact lens. A green ring was around the beacon and a red ring around the lighthouse, and every star showed a painter's impressionist night of light split and swirling when bright enough. To see her without a blurry halo, I got closer and she kissed me, a kiss that didn't end until there were four thousand rings above us in the blueness of a moonless sky.

My life soon made it to her mouth. I thought of fusion reactions and heavy water, physics take on some physical entendre under the interplay of our bodies in motion. How long it went on I cannot know. Twenty minutes, fifty minutes, whatever the span of our entanglement, I came to the surface to find the Hindenburg exploding over her Saxon nose. Only the medication could explain how I withheld myself, or how it withheld me, from coming when only a virgin. Apparently what I took was Soma and Tantra.

"I need to put this fire out before we burn too fast and there's nothing left of us," Gisele said, and she slid off her sweater and her shirt and her tights and her skirt. Three steps forward, passing just out of a street lamp's beam, shedding her underwear on the shore. Her body was better than my sticky blanket visions.

"It's April!" I shouted. I was supposed to be the suicidal one whom the other would heal, and now we hadn't just switched roles, we were playing the same one. How is a man already drowning supposed to come to the rescue of a woman with rocks in her pockets? At least Gisele was naked and couldn't sink herself like the writer she loved the most.

"Come on, John!"

I hesitated. I could feel her nose twitch even though I couldn't see it. What witchery was this that pulled my legs forward, as they had been once pulled by the devil in the woods? They were walking themselves toward her in the water.

Dry World

"Come darling. Come," and I abandoned my past, as well as a button down, a sweater, and underwear as I had lost my pants an hour before. I was escaping my madness and entering hers and it felt as sharp as the lake attacking me. Its temperature pounded my smoker's lungs. Through my gasps, I rasped this chorus as if it were in incantation that could transport us safely back to land and dry us as if this had never happened. I chanted:

> All I feel is what's real
> All I feel is what's real
> All I feel is what's real
> All I feel is what's real

I stayed in only long enough to find her in the blackness of night water and pull her shivering form to the shore, where, wrapped in the blanket, back in car, we shared a bucket seat with the heat vents roaring over us, and, though we were naked, there was too much coldness within us to do anything more than warm each other. As I held her writhing body in my still quaking arms, I convinced myself that I could save her from herself, but only if I stayed closer to her than I could if I were to remain in Roosevelt, writing on my own. I would give her a reason to live as she had just given me one. We would save each other, a lie that felt true because it was simpler and more elegant than the complications of reality.

We didn't make love that night, but we signed a pact with bracing whispers. I would move back to Ann Arbor, and we would be lovers from then on.

Chapter 7

More Potent than the Ocean

New York

With Billie in the apartment, it took me until dawn to sleep. I awoke from dreams of dunes at midday. I had skipped my meds and already there was a sense of wrongness. There was no design behind the missed dose. The reason for going without was simple: by the time I remembered to take them it was already so late that I was afraid I wouldn't wake up should my boss call the next morning. My boss did call the next morning. Plenty of times I had missed my medication without any significant consequences, and yet I had never fallen in love without a far more serious destabilization than drugs or lack thereof could account for. Between the skipped dose and the new girl, I had a feeling madness was inevitable, and that anticipation is usually worse than the madness itself.

Billie had vanished by the time I left my bedroom. I was too drowsy to be upset just yet. A phone call had roused me before I could go through my morning routine. Usually I prayed on my knees to stay sober, then brewed coffee and headed out to the balcony to smoke a cigarette or two, until the percolation could be heard chirping through the open kitchen window. At least once a week, Roger Abbey broke this routine with an early morning phone call. This was one of those mornings, and between the lack of medication, the onset of infatuation, and the interruption of routine, I could feel these forces nudging the gyroscope into a crooked cycle. Roger was already spinning. I had introduced him to

Dry World

Red Bull and the old man would down a few each morning, so that by the time he called me his words were buckshot sprays of piercing ideas in all directions. But it always started with the weather report.

"I haven't been outside yet. This girl I met last night isn't in the bathroom, and you woke me just now," I said. Roger had me writing about the weather every day and emailing it to him, this to the end that I pay close and consistent attention to what was going on outside of myself. What an extraordinarily difficult assignment for someone as narcissistic as I am. I would stand outside, scrawling into what I called, "The Elizabeth Street Journal" and do as I was instructed. I was to write precise descriptions of the world around me without involving anything that Roger would arbitrarily construe as emotion. This he called assignment one.

"And where are you with assignment three?" Roger asked.

I was also on a quest to discover why I wanted to write, why I would bother throwing pages on to the towering pile of babble, what was driving me to create, and it seemed to go back to my very purpose as a human being. "I have another answer," I said. "Let me know if this one is bullshit too." I told him I wanted to write because I could give voices to the many people who would otherwise never have them.

"You're going too far up your own ass again John. At least Narcissus didn't drown in shit. It's about time we met." We agreed to head to the terrible diner between us, where I always got a burger with a neon stream of liquid guacamole and Roger always got three pieces of pie. The Midnight Diner would let us sit out front where Roger would smoke filtered cherry cigars. I would offer him cigarettes out of pity, which he would refuse until just before he left. Mr. Abbey always took one for the road. In the meantime, it was coffee, coffee and coffee. I needed to be roused and headed there early. The burger was gone by the time Roger showed and I was well into a fresh pack of smokes. The place was liberal enough to let us smoke them at the tables outside.

"I'll give you a hint on number three. John, why are you sober? Answer that and you'll answer why you write. So?" I stuttered and tried to talk about the new girl, but he drove the hook in deeper. "Do you even read your Big Book?" The Big Book was AA's bible.

Brian and I had read a chapter about the effects of alcoholism on families only a few days before. I told him I could quote it better than he could even though he had twenty-seven years sober, and he agreed but insisted my recitations were meaningless without full knowledge of the motives behind them.

"What about that line where they say, 'We cannot solve the riddle?'"

"You keep fishing and you're never going to shoot a deer."

Roger was fond of sententious riddles that sounded profound only because it was a famous writer saying what might otherwise sound banal. I took one of his cigars without asking and lit it. We bottomed out our coffee cups at the same time and he told me a story about the writer Primo Levi. Roger was fond of recapitulating passages of Holocaust related writings and looking for meaning in evil in general. I was helping research a novel about a kid from North Roosevelt who had murdered his whole family on the day after Thanksgiving. That's how I got to New York City: as simple as answering an ad in the Roosevelt Register.

The waitress brought the pot back around, and Roger blew cherry smoke in her direction and then apologized three times, at one point patting her hand while finishing his background on the Jewish writer and cutting into the meat of the anecdote.

"He said, if two paths diverge in the wood, and you try to take them both, you end up lost in the woods between." He tucked in his chin and wrinkles folded his neck into rolls. That neck was the only fat part of his body.

Roger was forty-two years old and sixteen novels into his career. John Updike was effectively his bitch, and that MacArthur fellowship only added to his clout. This man could create or destroy me. Sometimes he just wanted someone to iron his collars at the laundromat. He even made me a flow chart I had to do it his way.

His other errands were never so anal and usually ended with a sense that I had completed a quest. It was time for another. He had the same explosion of curly hair that I did, except for his was pure white, and his anxious mannerism was two twist it around his finger as a teenage girl might. I was more likely to rub my poof until is stuck up from static. We were each playing with our hair when he gave me my mission. He needed ivory.

"There's a dealer in front of the Apple Store on Prince and Greene who will pull it out from under his table if you mention sandworms. I need to feel ivory to describe the skin of a woman. Here is a thousand dollars. Get what you can and await further instructions. Oh, and do you mind if I have one of those light Cigarettes? My throat needs a break." He dropped a twenty on the table, handed me a grand, bounded into traffic, and then climbed into a cab on Lafayette without bothering to ask if he could keep on smoking. The cab stalled behind a roaring delivery truck for a minute or two, and I watched him stare straight through me as if I were only the anonymous extra in the background of a story far more important than my life. I chased his whims and sometimes I even caught them.

Only then did I realize that I had not reported to him at all on assignment number two. This assignment, my research into the theories behind violence and aggression from a neuroscience perspective, left me holding a bag full of late nineteenth century alienist writings on emotion that predated Freud and originated with William James only about a mile from where I stood, but a hundred plus years before. My day was fucked. It was only a matter of time until I would have to get in a cab and meet him at Karma, on Third Street and First Avenue, where he would be writing and chaining cherry cigars together. I had to plan my whole day around being able to drop everything and meet him. And I was supposed to work in an hour.

There was no explaining to a piddling manager at a Starbucks that the greatest writer of his generation would fire me if I didn't meet him with stacks of copies I had made of rare psychological texts. So I called and told them I had a complete nervous breakdown and would need a week off to go to the hospital. I knew they couldn't legally fire me and I knew by then that the breakdown wasn't even a lie; it was an inevitability. I could feel its grip around the pleasure receptors in my synapses. The transmitters were sending me and I would have liked to have blamed Billie, or Roger, or both, but there was no use blaming someone else for a state only I could resolve. At that point I decided to sleep with my ringer on and wait to spring at the fickle whims of my master. The ivory could wait until my brain was working again. Home was east, Ivory, to the West. I turned north to wander. My thoughts were a genetic algorithm in reverse, producing only the fittest sort of madness. There was infinity in Gaussian distribution of finite iterations. I would never be well enough. I needed my meds, but did I want them?

There was Billie, ending all other thought, standing across Lafayette, a cup of rice pudding in her bony hand. Why was she here now? I was too pleased to care. She hadn't changed from the night before: the same vest, jeans, and boots. Between the two taxis I skipped. By the time I reached her, her backpack was unzipped, and she was rooting through. Unable to free her hands, she went for a kiss. You would think I'd notice that she tasted like powdered sugar and incense ashes. And I did, I did, but I also noticed the spaces between her teeth. I thought, as I tasted her, that even her dentistry resembled Gisele's.

Inside her tattered knapsack, I could see toiletries, a phone charger, laptop, underwear, socks, and a tattered copy of Dune. She understood what I was seeing. "Always be ready to hit the road," she said. I brushed Billie's cheek with my thumb. Billie pulled her pack back around her shoulder and patted my stroking hand with a soft palm.

"Let's move to Michigan together," I said.

She took my arm, and, interlaced, we strolled. She took out her player and split the headphones. We listened to the honeyed voice of a mellow woman plucking her guitar. She smiled, spacey teeth gleaming in the high white sun. I placed a cigarette in her mouth and lit it. Her lips contained fire.

"You're ready," I said.

"What?"

"To move to Roosevelt."

"When I marry you my mom will buy us a co-op," she said. Nose twitch. I kissed her top self cheek.

"Who are we listening to?"

"Billie Schlegel." And my love sang this into the bud of my right ear:

Maybe I'm flirty
Really I'm kind
Their thoughts are dirty
I know the mind
Maybe I'm teasing
Really I'm scared
Just cause I'm pleasing
Don't think I share
Your intense emotion
Where did you get the notion
My pheromones are potion
More potent than the ocean
Men! I'm overwhelmed with men!
I tell them time and again
I'm their friend

Dry World

"Who wrote that?" I asked. She softly slapped my shoulder. I released her arm and ran ahead, still hand in hand, dragging her, not even knowing where we were going, only the direction, west. "Manifest Destiny!" I shouted. Billie followed, her flat heels clacking behind me until I felt a hundred bony pounds hit my broad back, and she was on my shoulders, we were piggy backing down Prince Street.

Willowy waif she might be but she felt like a sack of cement. I crouched to let her off and collapsed. And there, on the white sidewalk, her on top of me, she put a dollop of rice pudding on my nose and licked it off. Took a drag and blew smoke in my face and blew my reserve to pieces. I kissed her, of course. Hard, then fluttering, then hard again. And only after, during her hydrogen laughter, did her evaporation recur to me. Where in the fuck had she gone? I walked in hand-held muteness until, halfway between Crosby and Broadway, I had to ask. "Where did you go this morning?"

"Brian called," she said. She'd grown a third arm and reached into my chest and bent my heart until it was just about to break. "I knocked on your door to see if you wanted to come with, but you didn't respond. I figured you were jerking off to the thought of me."

I was so love-drunk, I didn't even drop her hand. We just kept walking. "Then I wrote for a couple of hours, waiting for the rice pudding place on Spring to open." And at that very moment, when we had reached Greene Street, I saw the devil: same gray bandana, same blue-gold eyes. My throat was dry. I thought of cold feathers in my shaking hands. Now the cardinal killer had followed me to New York. The middle-aged meddler who'd walked over the moonlight on Lake Michigan was back in business. He was the one with the vendor's table in front of the Apple store.

"What's wrong?"

A shiver ran from my hand up hers.

"I'm sorry," she said.

"Not you." A night without medication and I was hallucinating. I could see the gold seem to spread in the gray man's eyes.

"That man looks just like…" she started.

I hadn't seen him since Paul's wedding. I thought he was through with me after destroying my life back then. He looked no older but somehow wiser and sadder because of this newly acquired wisdom. "How do you know him?" I asked, dropping her feathery hand in astonishment.

"I have dreams about the future and he is always there at the end, like a talk show host summing up the point of the vision." And I couldn't bear to tell her that he was a hallucination, that there couldn't be a devil, and that it meant we were of the same sickness. Of course we were. We were both insane. Folie a deux. But beyond that, I have noticed that only so many people can see the Devil. When they do, it always means that they are very, very eccentric. I forced myself to forget everything but lust and jealousy.

"What were you doing with Brian?"

Billie didn't answer. She approached the gray man. I stayed where I was, paralyzed by fear, and felt abandoned for the second time. Billie picked up a white knife, curved like the tip of a tusk, and ran a bony finger across the sharpened blade. Over the din of the tourists, all I could make out was his refusal to sell. Only after he made her laugh did the Devil look at me, the gold in his eyes coating me with molten metal to make me more beautiful through pain, and then he winked.

I approached, Billie didn't get anywhere with him until I said, "Sandworms" and he asked if I had a thousand and one stories for the sultan. I handed him the envelope from Roger and pocketed the knife. Apparently the one she had first handled was being held for another customer, I was told. A kid with dreadlocks and robot tattoos.

I heard only this, just the first words she said, before I had to run, feeling pulled by a string on the chest again. Billie didn't catch up with me until I was halfway to Houston Street. From her smile it was clear she was enjoying what only seemed like a game.

"He's the real deal," she said. "An ivory dealer. Is that even legal?"

"Billie, he's my enemy. Stay the fuck away from him." I expected Billie to take offense, but instead she took my hand.

"John, he's not just your enemy. You're still shaking."

"Medication," I half-lied. Withdrawals and fear were hard to differentiate. "Let's get the fuck out of this godforsaken neighborhood."

"The one train's on Houston," she looked behind us, as if concerned we were being followed.

"What's on the one?" I asked, looking back myself.

"My place," she said, and the spaces between ivories widened as I kissed her.

Chapter 8

All The World's a Class

Michigan

Eugene O' Neill Cooperative House stood in a double lot atop a gentle Ann Arbor hill. The white house had the decaying grandeur and expansive grounds of a former plantation. A young forest had grown in a front yard untended for decades. Nestled behind skinny beech trees, bushes, and an ancient spruce, this mansion stood ten feet over the highest treetops. Eugene O' Neill served its highest-shelf beverage first, and it was enough to get you drunk on beauty. Yes, besotting the visitor was a verandah that ran the length of the front, a half circle with a thirty-foot radius. Pillars and a curving railing enclosed this space. Seven steps rose to double doors. Two pairs of papery couches lined the perimeter. A porch swing hung too high on the far right. The smell of a freshly tapped keg rose from the unpolished floorboards on that humid morning. Usually there was someone sitting and chilling, smoking or studying, boozing or tweaking, but the place had been empty when I entered. My feet had clacked across dingy hardwood planks as I'd passed unseen into the memories of my three years there, forward into a future where love seemed to last.

The foyer always smelled as if it had been mopped with malt liquor, mere beer being to weak to be as pungent as that place smelled. There was an acid dealer in the basement. There was fifty-cent Pabst in the Coke machine. This had never been the place for a sober man, and it was no wonder that I went on dry emotional benders here, living through the vicarious highs of indulging coeds.

I had stayed only to keep meeting women, and as I had met first
Chloe and then Gisele through the draw of our space, I told myself
that my jag through nightlife where I never quite belonged had
been worth its weight in pussy. I was ready to drink what I never
had, for that first sip of Absinthe, for the visions of Gisele to hunt
down my mind, drunk and shooting crooked. It was time to ingest
the liquid drug that had detained me in this sordid place too long
already.

I used to tell myself I stayed because I had something to
teach my friends. The lessons and lectures I gave were often met
with boredom, but less so when I sang them. Lyrics came to mind
that day:

> I'm a teacher
> All the world's a class
> But good teachers
> Learn from what they ask
> I'm a student
> When it comes to you
> And good students
> Learn from what they do

A burgundy leather suitcase I had yet to put down on my
old floor weighed my left arm. I released it from my place on her
bed and it clunked into a point of rest. A vinyl garment bag that
contained the tux I would wear to my older brother's upcoming
wedding swished across my hard plastic guitar case as it slid to the
shiny floor. I was messing the place up in advance. Where was
Gisele if not there to welcome me?

My old room was strangely the same. The same pair of
Lichtenstein prints, the same short story scrolling across the wall

above the same mattress, no box spring, the same brown easy chair and the same peach loveseat. What had changed: surfaces, her books neatly packed in the hardwood crates, her lavender sheets stretched tight across the bed, her clothing in the closet. Also, everything was cleaner, and the floor was shinning, spitting back the direct sunlight through windows spotted not by even the slightest smudge. I saw my reflection and my shadow and thought of the Devil in gray. Turning away, I entered a closet tightly organized without the normal outcroppings of my wrinkled garments. I buried my nose in a T-shirt on a hanger that smelled only of detergent and fabric softener. But I did find her fragrance rising from the dell of her bed, where I fell into a fraudulent sleep. I just did not know how she'd feel when she finally arrived. Would she be scared to find me not in some distant town, but here preset in her present, moved into her new home?

I crossed the threshold into the mild hallucinations known just before sleep. Outside the door there was the jangle of brass penetrating the lock, and a creak of hinges singing like a beetle pushing the sun, the viscous fluids of men singing out the melodies of yesterday as the shit was pushed through the heavens. She had arrived, and I smelled the intoxicating smoke of her sweat on that hot day from across the room. She saw me and stripped anyway, ripping the clothes off herself as a frustrated man might peel the label of his forty-ounce beer. She was naked and in a towel before I could rise.

I was told to shower too but I said nothing. I stayed in bed and feigned sleep. She left me there and I waited. I stunk to her. I always stunk to her. She folded her socks for Christ's sake. I couldn't see the filth she could. There were scents only her and dogs knew. I could smell nothing but her. I was still in her bed, after all. When she entered again, already dry, having blown her hair into a Hollywood simulacrum of womanhood, I made a few specious moves toward her other towel and then pulled the towel off her body.

Gisele's breasts had a conical point to the pertness. The nipples on them were small, the size of nickels, their tips peaking out of flatness like pink mesas. I pushed one tip down and watched snap back into place as if it were a short spring. She took a catholic kneel with her towel padding her knees. On me she would prey. After unfolding the red canvas belt through the steel hoops that held it together, she threw it and those hoops clanked twice, first when they hit the wall and then when they hit the hardwood floor. Then it was down with my tight jeans, down with such force that the denim roughed up my skin. I felt as though I were being sanded to smoothness so that I could be stained with a finish of sweat. My boxers had been pulled off by my jeans and so there hung the few inches of my flaccid cock. She looked at me as if she were offended by my lack of excitement.

"Medications," I said.

"I can cure that," she said. Her thinness made me look and feel larger than I was and I liked that. The same small hands that had pressed my palms perhaps a month before were now where I wanted them, giving my life life.

I was with her on the cusp of Olympus, naked as Ancient Greece. The pressure to win was there. She expected a medal of skin shining under sun and the anthem of her cries. I wanted to sing through her hair of our independence from everyone else. Our dancing competition somewhere between the burn of gym mats and the chill of ice rinks. Ours would substitute for a battle, settling scores and then wiping their numbers clean until there was only blankness in our minds.

But fuck the metaphors when it comes to Gisele. The cutting arc of thighs squeezed the best of me into pinches with punches of her thinness on my every curve. I could be a camera that captured all the senses and I would do her no justice, for this would never happen this way again and anything but the first variation would fade in impact like a tactile echo. In places she had bones where I had known imperfections in others. The way she played with me was a perfect improvisation. Our instruments were our thighs and hands and anything else we could move in concert with each other. There was no language in me for what I felt or anything else, only the music of skin percussion and her soaring cry.

It was evening and spring and the sun was the crimson arc of storm forecast out the window beyond her. I fixed my eyes on it as if I could capture all its creativity within me and make her and the rest of the universe new with the right kind of clench. Just then she rolled away from me and my arm threw itself into a cruel reflex and grabbed her shoulder, and squeezed it and pounded her back against the mattress hard, so hard that she bounced a bit but even that I cut short as I pinned her, and she was a dead butterfly, utterly transformed from what she had been and captured at the peak of her beauty and pinned, and pinned, and pinned again with a shaft to the cork. Sometimes I can almost find words for her.

As if reading the warped grooves of my expression with the needle of the finger teasing my cock, and I was turning so far as my head would spin, Gisele played a classic I did not know and I was ready to sing to her when the conceit ended with a sharp slap. What she read bothered her. Somehow through the pulses whose communication predates spines she felt my mind and wanted me to know that she was not about to flutter into the jar of my domestic dreams. When the third slap came it was followed at once by her throwing me back and riding me as if I were her new legs, stronger legs, legs that could win her any race, a gift from the Gods to be used in some twisted fate we could not yet know.

With Gisele it always felt like a competition for who could display more pleasure for the other. She would massage me to the point of explosion and then pulse against her will above me and not on me by a force of will I still cannot understand. There is nothing sexier to me than almost getting off, but only if I eventually do. So she brought to the point of exhilaration, my hands up and a ribbon breaking over my chest, only to call off the race and run the damn thing again. Sometimes when drunk on wine and watching what stars I can see in this city I really believed that God made us together as one body and were only now doing his will. She had the kind of stammering mouth on her womb that could almost speak as its lips licked me, and sometimes I really heard it tell myths of conception on the scale of the stars, while her light fused the two of us into a thermonuclear test. Maybe it was the big and banging creation that was more real than any fable or fairy story for those never show the prince waist-deep in the princess, the crown and the slippers underneath his back and pinching it with every pulse against him. I am that prince and Gisele was that princess and we had done too well to care how that sounded. We only know that

Dry World

there are moments of release so bracing that it feels as though there is a childish resolution wrapping up the ends of our nerves into fists thrown aloft in exultation, where we were gods at the end of the games. I never did come though. I only groaned a proposal of marriage.

The rain came fast on the panes, squirting through the screen and spattering on our still body. It was still cool at night. The sun hung still through the prisms of droplets. I had seen snow on a sunny day only a month before, when I first knew that I had to leave college to get well, and yet here I was bedding a woman was more important than sanity. We stayed there, softened to a liquid as the rain flowed into her left flow of a body and all over the right of mine.

The last soft thunder rustled more than rumbled in the distance, Thor and Zeus now wrestling elsewhere. Gisele kissed my cheek as her nipples grazed my arm. Then she stood in all her thinness and remained still, until a wet gust hit and spattered us with the mist of raindrops shattered against a screen. There was a lull that even seemed to let the jostling tree limbs come to rest. Water was still moving but there was no more pattering, only the drips and flushes of water running off of the house. Gisele drowned even these as she put on a folk record.

I brushed a bit of wetness off of my cheek and my hand came up red from blood. Her cut my cheek somehow. I looked down, saw blood on the sheets, and wiped the fresh red from my hands. This left four long blotches from each of my fingers. Gisele was the kind of woman for whom stained bedding would be something of a crisis. Yet as the strums pulsed from my floor speakers, she wobbled as if on Olympus Mons and still getting used to low Martian gravity.

"John Rook," she said, "if you aren't true to me I swear to God I will die and take you with me. So when you say you want to marry me, just know that. Know that your life and mine are in your big old hands."

I would remember that first time as Mars remembers water, preserving its impressions because no further drops fell to wash them away. I have not had sex since Gisele, and there were none before her. My world is dry and will stay preserved because of it.

Chapter 9

You Were My Queen

New York

On a side street in the high seventies, just around the corner from Broadway, stands Billie's building. The bay window on her first floor studio overlooks the street like a balcony. For a while, we got no further than cement steps of her stoop. The sun had toasted the concrete until it was warm and buttery under our seats. We were ready to wake up to each other.

The pedestrians didn't exist. The callers on the other ends of our ringing phones didn't exist. The Devil with the blue gold eyes we had bought ivory from didn't exist. The wild children we would meet later, across town, didn't exist. Brian, the rousing monster whom she had awakened as a petulant child might tease an alligator, not knowing that its torpor belied deadly power, even he didn't exist. The millions around us and the billions on earth and the zillions of stars were just lint in our pockets to be discarded because we had found what we were really looking for.

Softly I sang for her while her foot tapped in time:

If you were my nurse
We'd never get worse
I'd never speak terse
I'd laud you in verse
I offer the entire world
If you would only be my girl

I let a silence hang after the song, then spoke: "When will we be grown up?"

"When someone turns thirty."

Could I wait six years? I couldn't even wait eighteen hours, let alone the three months I was supposed to put love aside until she had one year clean and sober. My sponsor and employer and mentor all in one wouldn't consider her utterly inappropriate and throw a cherry butt at me. But he wasn't on the street with us, and even God felt too weak to stop us from conjoining.

"You'll be twenty-six." I stroked the red streak in her hair.

"John, darling, let's get married then."

I squeezed the bones of her spry fingers. Joy I never knew with Gisele. Here was a bottled spirit, ready to grant wishes when rubbed.

"Promise me," she said.

"Living where?" Billie freshened this game of futures.

She released my hand and reclined, supporting herself with her long arms, spreading featherweight across each narrow palm. "The steps are hot."

"There are twelve of them, you know."

I counted a laughed.

"We need room for our family." Past the stoop a mother passed with twins.

"Brooklyn?" I asked, thumbing her high-boned chin. Possession possessed me. I wanted the whole set of her china skin. I continued: "A brownstone would be good enough for Billie Cosby."

"The outer boroughs? What about the riff raff?" She held half my face as if I were a tender melon about to drop to the floor, sweet and overripe and thus fragile. She was as worldly as Gaia compared to me. Her mother's private jet was waiting for us always. Billie's eyes closed over maize and blue irises, and she shook her head hard, as if rocking or rocking out. She added that no one famous lived outside of the Dakota.

"Roger Abbey lives in Park Slope, and he's better than anyone."

"I have to meet him."

"According to the New Yorker, yes, the New Yorker."

"What was the book of his that Charlie Kaufman adapted?"

"When I'm a famous rock star we won't need your mom's money." A truck roared by her stoop, blaring a guitar anthem from decades past. Britain was serenading us from a lorry.

I looked into the unlit window of her apartment, taking solace in its bay while wondering how much her mother paid for it.

Billie sat up and took my chin in her hand, brought my face back to her direction. I took this hand and sucked a knuckle. The affect of her eyes was photoelectric, charging every atom of her copper skin with their light.

"When we have our kids," I said when her fingers left my mouth, "we're moving to Michigan. We don't want them growing up like you."

"Fuck you. I'm from nowhere."

"A book for everywhere and nowhere?"

"Thus spoke Rook. Michigan why?" Her finger slid for my mouth but missed twice and had to enter on a third try. "I'll never let you stop touring."

"Baby swaddled in view of the rock?"

"Double bill. Turns playing and holding the kids." An open-eyed kiss. Photon after photon hit, their virtual mass showering me infinitesimally as the gravity of my arrogance bent them around me. Forget mechanistic equations. There was no model for love. Such force within me. I could understand general relativity well enough to know that power is the theory of everything, bent only by the virtual mass of love. Heavy light reveries clouded my mind with electrons and bullshit. With her in my mind I knew who began the big bang. And in them, my reflection looked better than it ever had.

"What would you name a son?"

Dry World

I thought: Brian. Suddenly I wanted to say the name aloud. I wanted to ask how close he was to Billie, and the jealousy gnawed at the cheese of my mania. Brian was green with jealousy and crazier than the moon. Moldy with ergot and unexpectedly intoxicating, the wielder of meat cleavers who chased people as sentences wear out their welcome with too many clauses, unless German, German cheese, he was capable of the worst. As falsely mild as an aged cheddar mistaken for a muenster. He was going to take a bite out of us both before we were through. Now I was chasing rays of light-speed tangents, my mind accelerating past reasonable barriers, a tachyon. "My mother's maiden name; I would name a son Morrison."

"We'd call him Morrissey." Nose twitch. "Our girl would be McNamara after my mother." And she began to sing of creation, as if our children were already in her arms: While God designed the appendix before Adam gave birth to Eve who had time for creation myths that even angels can't believe. I've had that kicking in my gut feelings for years. We should finish it."

"To make life took a billion years to make love takes less than six days so why when my life's in arrears do I seek out your secular grace?" I suggested.

She brought her arms together and rocked an imaginary infant. The baby in her arms felt as real as the future we were sure to share. The way she carried his weight. The way he held out his arms. The way she nursed it with her finger. She handed him to me.

"You could be Billie McNamara instead of Billie Schlegel?"

Her head neared my lap as if she were cooing to the phantom child, and while my dick filled with blood, she replied, "I might use it as a stage name." She laid her head across my denim waist, as if listening to the private language of our twins so intently as to write a dictionary of their mumblings. I could hear the heart beat in my brain.

"What if you're Billie Rook?"

"Darling, my dad would love you," she said, pulling my Clark Kent curl as if it were a spring that could lift us into outer space. I got more excited. "You'd just whip out your songs and he would know you were Romany."

"Can we name our second daughter Romany?"

"Don't get ahead of this baby. It needs to know it is loved before we get around to more." She rocked her arms and brought their virtual baby to my face that I might kiss it. And the child was there and he had eyes of blue and gold, so tight was that Dark Lord's grip on my synapses.

Thankfully she was quick to distract me from my madness. She pulled out her player and I heard something she'd recorded with the microphone on her laptop. A harmonica. Banshees battling with a bat family in the best possible way – her father was an artist with perfect ears and a penchant for the night and getting high. Wailing, weeping boogie of high blown blues.

The thought of her father had cooled me off. I popped her earbud out of my left canal and wiped the orange wax off of the white headphone. Billie plucked the chunk out of my hand and the cherubs grew wings, red on the blue yellow and white on the blue and they fluttered about us as she slid the earwax into her pocket. Then they dashed off at a speed that blurred everything around us, as if some light-speed barrier had been broken by my fantasy. I had seen the future by traveling without moving.

"You know I love you," I said. Her face close, a flecked nose flickering, her eyes surpassed the splendor of the stars above it

"I love you." We had known each other for less than twenty-four hours. We held each other, my nose buried in her tea-tree scented hair. All I saw was auburn shadows that reminded me of Gisele, but only for long enough to forget the rain of that first time and look to the sun. A shiver passed from Billie's body to mine and I pulled her closer, until her breast was my chest. The chain reaction was ready to burst the Hudson wind into a curtain of pseudo-sunlight, conflagrating everything in the napalm of life. I could smell gasoline that afternoon. "Let's get somewhere with our lives," she said, and we'd known each other for less than nineteen hours when, hand in hand, we entered her apartment to fuse.

Billie changed into a pretty print skirt that I never saw after that afternoon, ample in length, olive, beneath a T-shirt, brown and lettered with darker brown, and to complete the color scheme, she had donned an olive scarf and was holding between pursed fingers a fragrant clove cigarette. She was not shod, however, for a meeting. And her umber backpack lay discarded near the guitar.

My heart beat like a sub-woofer as she sat down, cool skirt billowing, contracting, on the loveseat next to me, and tipped her odorous clove in the muddied crystal ashtray.

With spry fingers she snatched the novel I had opened. Quickly, unfettered by the half-burnt clove she held, Billie flipped violently through the pages in search of something she wished me to see. I brought my head so close that red streak touched my jaw and her arm brushed my china chin as brought clove back to her lips. "The conjurer had poured milk, molasses, foaming champagne into a young lady's new white purse..."

"And lo, the purse was intact," I finished from memory. She was no nymphet. She was a woman. I whisked the dirty book away. She grabbed for it. I moved it out of reach. She tumbled onto me. She caught me by her lithe, tattooed wrist. "Read," she said.

"COWARDICE" she had, tattooed on her, "is the worst vice."

The novel escaped to the floor like a fluttering cardinal. She set down the clove, and lay me back into the right-hand corner of the loveseat. Then, the impertinent woman extended her hand across my lap.

By this time, I was insane, yet still cunning. Lying there on the sofa, I brought my lust into her guileful hands. Singing fast, catching up with her winded breath, she cooed the lyrics to the song I'd first played her on the walk to my apartment. We are gonna be the stars going to them in your car through the church and then the bar something something my guitar. She kept repeating these fragments of my self-love anthem, the song of ourselves, filling in the lines she couldn't remember but keeping the rhyme scheme. She was musical and cinnamon as the spice mélange. Her hands twitched like surfacing sandworms and the sun was inside us, a desert sun impossibly bright and representing deaths large and little. Her hands twitched a little as they moved across my now bare lap; I stroked them, there she sprawled around me, Billie the blue screw, twisted by driver, a tongue first, there would be no intercourse ever with her but that seemed impossible then, as impossible as a love affair begun that fast that could ever last, last longer than a carton of the brand of cloves she was still consuming, singing through its puffs, losing her scarf, rubbing the skin of her scarfless neck across my nose, the piled novels on the loveseat scattering onto the floor in a rattle as I writhed – and every stroke she gave, every shuffle and ripple, corresponded between my bursting beast and the beauty of her agile fingers on my exposed cock.

Under dancing fingertips, I felt the thin hairs tingle to attention along her calves. She turned to discard her burnt-out clove into the tray, her slight weight, her thighs and bottom, shifted atop my face and I found nothing beneath the skirt. I came into this welcoming darkness and the salt lake became a sea during an ice age, concentrated by the phase resolution of immense glaciers and saltier than it had ever been. Thus I entered a place where nothing mattered except the joy flowing from our bodies. What had begun as my novel play became a luminous tingle which reached a state of pure confidence found nowhere else in consciousness. With our mingling juices nearing that ultimate spasm, I slowed down to prolong the candelas. The sun pulsed behind a partial eclipse of lunar shadowy lunacy, I was mad for her, we were as united as the trinity of phases and Christianity and as alone as Christ arising for

Magdalene. I watched her milky, ash-flecked, beyond the pale of my
contained thermonuclear reaction, aware of the fusing atoms, yet
chaining the reactions like popcorn at Christmas, sentimentally and
nostalgic for past joy while still experiencing the pleasure of the
present, and the sun was on her hips, streaming through the
translucent skirt, and her lips were still singing my song, now with
all the words in place, but these I barely heard. Everything in its
right place. Pleasure flung wide like Blake's doors and Urizen was
rising. The least flicker would gain the paradise of the primuum
mobile beyond the beyond. Paused at the cusp of a joyous abyss, an
infinite fall that felt like flying, I kept repeating stray words – star,
church, pride – until I fell, the first anything but penetration had
brought my med-paddled body to climax, as I feasted on her
creases, that the buzz might bring her great gasps to stutter her
singing voice, and because of her absent underthings, there was
nothing to prevent my thumb from joining the fun inside her tent
and massage the gravity well of her groin, and she wiggled, and
squirmed, as might radiation rarefacting through the Van Allen
Belt, and she wiggled, and squirmed, as might a tickled foot, and I
remembered that memories are sometimes involuntary, as the
shadow of Gisele's identical genitals pursed through my
consciousness until Billie crushed out my thoughts from ecstasy
whose high notes I knew no bird could sing.

Immediately afterward, she rolled off and answered her
phone. There she stood and winked, cheeks shining, skirt crinkled
and sodden, her eyes passing over me heavily as the sun as she
listened and spoke (to Brian who was telling her to meet him in
Central Park later that night and to bring a butcher knife and who
knew if he were joking), she kept swinging the scarf she'd once cast
aside until it blurred into a brown circle of dark matter barely

glowing. When she hung up, she spoke nothing of every word I'd heard, said only, "Let's go to that meeting."

Chapter 10

Pretenses Disguise the Dumb

Michigan

The father who has now arrest me is my only doctor, and, no matter how far away I am, he still makes house calls. I am honest with him, perhaps too honest, so when he heard that Gisele and I were hosting a potluck cocktail party, his reaction was to get in his station wagon and drive the two hours from Roosevelt to Ann Arbor to rescue me from sure relapse. He called as Gisele and I were on our way home from the liquor store. We had bought a fifth of Jack Daniels, which had been my favorite choice when I still drank. Gisele had gone three months without a drink. I assumed this meant she just didn't like booze. So there I was, years away from my last drop of alcohol, a bottle in one hand, and my father's voice piping out of the other.

"You're out of control, John."

"Paul's coming to the party." My older brother's very name angered my father.

"You're with him right now, aren't you?"

"Dad, I do all the right things and then I do one thing and all the trust I should have is..." Impishly, my love massaged my crotch. I swatted at her hand but missed. She took and held it.

Dry World

"Trust? John, you're in a mixed state and you know how dangerous that is. I'm glad you're partying down in Ann Arbor."

"Oh, sarcasm is real helpful." I wanted to strangle my father with the magnetic fields binding us. "Listen, Dad, I've got to meet up with Paul. He's coordinating this fine event."

"You're this close to being the same no good drunk he is, John." I could see his hairy knuckles pinching the air. "And I can't let that happen. Not when you're so close to graduating."

"I am graduated for all purposes. And now I want to have fun, but I'm not going to drink today. That's all I can promise."

"I'm coming to get you." Gisele heard this and raised an auburn eyebrow. "If you're done with school you're done with that town."

"I'm with Gisele now and I don't have time for this, Dad." I was too deluded to feel his concern. I was having a ball with my girl and that was all that mattered. "I guess if you want to come to the party that could be fun."

"I'll see you in three hours." The old man drove slow. I actually looked forward to his coming. My condition had been improving. I felt more centered and stable than I had in the weeks before, and even my brother agreed that the worst for me seemed to have passed. This only made me more dangerous.

Paul stood on the circular porch of O' Neill with Jim Harrison, the guy who was going to be his best man in a week. The two were such close friends that they were often mistaken for a couple, and Paul spent more time drinking with Jim than he did with his fiancé. "Where's Jill?" I asked.

Paul shrugged, as if he cared far more about the booze in my hand than his future wife.

Jim grinned. He stood six and a half feet and was the handsomest devil I have ever seen. "In the kitchen where she belongs, making horse derves," he said.

"I don't like him," Gisele said to me, as if only I could hear. She even pointed at Jim.

"Dr. Rook will be joining us this fine evening," I said.

"Jesus, John," said my brother. "What did you say this time?"

"He thinks I'm going to get drunk."

Paul nodded. He always thought I should. I suspect he still missed having me as a using buddy.

"I'll get drunk for you," Gisele said. She cracked the fifth of Jack Daniels and did me the courtesy of swallowing before kissing my mouth. The taste made me cringe from its cloying joy, but what I really noticed was that she didn't cough. That scared me. Jim and Paul smiled approvingly.

Paul brought his fingers to his lips, asking for a cigarette. "Who's coming?"

"Your dad," I said, handing him a smoke.

"What kids are coming?" Jim rubbed his short blond hair. His basketball star's hands were so big they made his head look under-scaled, a fact I noted with some satisfaction. Pinhead.

"Charlie's bringing a fifth of Malibu," I said. "Simon's bringing a fifth of Beefeater, and Colin's bringing a gallon of Vodka."

"Girls, John, what girls?" asked Jim. His fingers pulled at eager lips.

"You're the only guy here without one of those," I said, perhaps too readily. Gisele laughed and pointed at Jim. She already seemed drunk. I wondered how far this would go.

"Fuck you both," Jim said. "I'm the most beautiful man in Michigan." This may not have been an exaggeration. Jim stroked his stubbly chin and said, "I'll just call Chloe and her girls. They love me."

This was a low blow. I had written more songs about Chloe than anyone, and she still told me that she loved me, though we were only ever friends. So I sang, in retort, disregarding the girlfriend at my side, disregarding the jeers from my brother before he slipped off the porch and into the co-op to be with his woman, I sang a song that once meant the world to me.

A day without Chloe's like a day without food
Possible supposing I don't care about my mood
Or instincts opposing the lifestyle of a man who'd
For some reason chosen to faithfully fast and brood
Without Chloe

I waited for a nose twitch but Gisele's was still except for its minute nostrils, flaring. "Chloe Downing? I hate that bitch. I can't believe you wrote a song about her."

"John, isn't your supposed novel about her, too?" said Jim. I wanted to destroy my old friend. I imagined a short fiction piece where Jim got date raped. As I had cut Chloe with my pen for only liking me while I loved her, so I planned to hurt Jim. But a fury truncated this revenge fantasy: Gisele shoved my shoulder with surprising strength. It was Jim's turn to point and laugh.

"She's your Beatrice? The bitch who wouldn't give me a radio show on the radio station?" Gisele took a long drink of whiskey without a wince. Then she stormed into the house, the porch door slamming behind her. I looked at my watch and counted down the hours until my father would arrive, then I followed her into the house to reconcile. When I found her, alcohol seemed to have cleaned her memory of offense, and we shared another whiskey kiss before I returned to the porch to wait for my friends.

The party itself was a clusterfuck. At first, Gisele was too busy getting drunk to unleash her Chloe fury just yet. My night came with waves of fear that at any moment, my beautiful friend would appear and there would be a cat fight on the veranda of O'

Neill. But Chloe hadn't spoken with me since Gisele. I missed her even as I hoped I would keep missing her.

Gisele hated her. Gisele hated almost all of my friends.

Charlie got red faced from booze before Paul called him his favorite gook. Because we had been friends since we were seven years old, I knew Charlie's family well enough to know his father had an amazing sense of humor when picking the name of a first born Vietnamese son, and Charlie knew my family well enough not to get rankled at my loutish brother's racial insensitivity. But when Gisele called my friend of fifteen years a banana (white on the inside, yellow on the outside) Charlie stormed off, his hands furiously clutching the crunch of his gelled, black hair.

Chloe didn't come, thank god, but some of her pretty friends did, and Gisele was openly cruel to them. She even spit whiskey in the face of Chloe's roommate. Most of it dribbled down Gisele's broad lips, but a few drops landed on the poor coed, who slapped Gisele. While I restrained my lover, her narrow body flailing in my flexed arms, Chloe's friend told me never to call Chloe again. I was left holding a writhing wreck who insisted on kissing me with bourbon breath.

My only friend whom Gisele liked didn't much like her. She bonded with Simon when he started strumming the right song on my guitar. They had a long conversation about the last track on a concept album about Anne Frank. But then she turned to me and said, "Why are none of your other friends worthwhile like this guy?" and Simon stopped playing. With a precise sweep of finger and thumb, he straightened the hedges of his eyebrows and thinned his lips until they all but disappeared. Then he disappeared, and I again I was left right where Gisele wanted me: alone with her.

By the time my father arrived everyone at the party was insanely drunk, with the exception of me. I was only insane. Dr. Rook stepped to me and sniffed my breath.

"You smell like Jack Daniels, John." His face was scowling our scowl.

"Gisele drinks that and kissed me." My father rolled his shallow sea eyes.

"Let's take a walk and talk," my father said, all but ignoring Paul's proximity. They barely spoke lest they start striking each other again.

"I swear on everything I believe I'm sober," I said. My father was much shorter than me, though he'd widened with age. He didn't walk so much as shuffle, hunched.

"You're not sober. You're dry." Dr. Rook shook his huge head, outsized for his stubby body. "This isn't sober, John, having cocktail parties."

"If I'm sober it's sober."

He paused in word and foot and sized me from head to toe. "For you, going off drugs is taking drugs. You're not sober to me."

Dry World

This hurt. I wanted to drink to whiskey back at the house and show him what drunk really was.

"You seem coherent." There was nothing so much as a pat on the shoulder, though – we're not that kind of family. "You're swinging, John. When was the last time you wanted to kill yourself?"

"When I got my grade on my Dante paper last month."

"That's not a normal reaction to a mediocre mark." As the leaves above us split open and revealed a faded stellar speckling, he straightened his gait. He was taking a clinical posture. "You are experiencing cognitive distortions. You're not safe. So I have to ask you," he hunched back into his stooping shuffle, "because I love you, and I don't want you to die, why, if you're done with school now, are you still here?"

From the hill where we stood, on a street corner, I looked only at the sienna sky, brightened at its corners by distant cities. "Just before George was born, I had a dream. Even twenty years hence I can't forget it." My father's scowl had tightened into a cold, clinical stare. He was analyzing me. I couldn't bear to watch that, so I found the brown sky and kept on with my story. "I stood atop a dune, one wave in a sea of desert. I was on a dry world, light years from earth. With me were two women: my mother and the love I have been looking for ever since. You and Paul were not there to beat me. I knew, as one can know only in dreams, that the girl beside would protect me from you and Paul. I felt safer than I ever have since."

"Now you're getting grandiose, John. 'Hence?' 'Atop?'"

I glanced back to my father and met eyes that caught flaxen flecks from the streetlamps. "Dad, listen to me. You're not able to hear. Gisele is the girl from the dream, Dad."

My father shook his slicked back head.

"No, listen to me. I love her. I need to be with her. I need to be in Ann Arbor."

My father folded, softened. The clinical scales had fallen from his balanced eyes. He stood up straight. "I had a dream about your mother before we met." I saw a photograph of a couple, lovely and loving. Clothes with the wide collars of another era. My parents at my age, when my father always walked erect. My parents got engaged when they'd known each other three weeks. They have been married ever since.

"I haven't had a drink today, Dad."

"I know, John. I know." We could hear the party before we finished walking around the block. There was a woman peeling open a can of laughter and a man screaming along to the lyrics of a rap explosion. "This might be the best place for you to have fun, but what about your career?" We reached the cement steps up to the old manor. "How are you going to finish a novel if you're doing this every night?" He pointed to the porch where his oldest son glared at us. Hatred had stiffened my brother's spine into a shaft. Straight, he stood and sneered. "It's time for me to go." There was definite fear in his quavering tone, as if the old man were thinking of those last blows he took from his son. "Paul can't do what he wants to do with me around." I knew he meant drugs and I knew then he'd given up as I'd never known him to. The fear only made the impending wedding more ominous. "I love you, John."

And I hugged my father on the steps, his Old Spice still wafting from the lapels of a dry pressed shirt. It felt like a hug after a spanking, hate and love each an arm. "I love you, Dad." Paul threw an empty bottle onto the grass beside us, but it didn't shatter, it landed only with a muffled thud. Gisele cackled. If our father heard this, he didn't acknowledge it, he didn't look back, he just shuffled into his station wagon and reddened the night with his taillights. I walked past them, brother and lover, into the house. There I took my medication and went into the deep sleep of the drugged. Alone in the bed, my eyes fluttered into a dream of a dry world and a future with a girl whose name I'd yet to learn.

Chapter 11

What Keeps You Still

New York

Outside a diner after the meeting, I wandered away from Billie to converse privately. My father and I spoke daily, but I had not talked to him since I had met my dream girl. While Billie spoke with some of the other kids milling and smoking on the Upper East sidewalk, I paced the west edge of First Avenue. Dad was calling on his cell phone, and it was late for him, so he could be only one place: the screened porch of our home. The only pockets of signal in the National Park were just outside the house. I pictured his pressed khakis, his checkered shirt, his mismatched tie loosened around a collar that couldn't hide his neck hair. All this pacing his hardwood verandah, a slouching gait that could have been motion captured from mine.

"Dad, how are you?"

"You sound strange." I imagined his furry fingers scrawling notes concerning my condition.

"I didn't get much sleep last night."

"How much?"

"None."

Dry World

A stethoscope materialized around his neck. He was more doctor than father now. "Did you take your meds?" A symphony of crickets scoring his words.

I paused and ran a hand through my wilderness hair. "I met a great girl."

"You didn't take your meds?"

In the City, an ambulance blurred, its siren shifting down in pitch. "Her name is Billie and she has the same three favorite books as me."

"So you got no sleep and you skipped your medication?"

"I was so excited." Two couture clad princesses clacked by, their outfits worth the price of my father's car. I looked at one and she looked away. I looked at the other and she smiled.

"What the hell are you doing out there, John?"

"We're going to Central Park to hang out after a meeting."

"You're going home to take your meds and then you're going to sleep." The miles between us seemed impossible to cross, as if we were speaking not just across three dimensions but four. Roosevelt was not just another place; it was another time.

"I have plans, Dad. With Billie." I knew he was telling me to take the next right action, I felt it in my heart, but my dick had vetoed the four-chambered parliament.

"I'm coming to get you." The miles of Ohio and Pennsylvania unfurled before me, distances endless compared to the density of the city. That he wouldn't even wait for morning worried me. I was endangering my father when I only wanted to endanger myself. "Your priorities are fucked, John. Fucked."

"Going to meetings is a bad thing?" I looked at the fuming riot of twittering kids horsing around.

"This shit you're pulling, the all night coffee and cigarettes, you might as well be drunk." I could hear his mind reciting the criteria for caffeine-induced psychosis.

My tone was stuttering into clipped rage. "Dad, I know how to take care of myself." He was right. I was wrong. Nothing got me angrier.

We were feeding off each other's fury. His blows got lower. "Remember Gisele?" I held the phone away from my quaking head. I was vibrating with pure fury. "Do you want that again?"

"Oh, right, take a scalpel to my scars." Ready to hang up, I turned around and paced back toward my gathered friends, most years younger than me.

"I'll be there in sixteen hours." The worst. He was coming. There was no stopping him once he made up his mind. I was an elder at this meeting. I couldn't let the young ones hear my dad treat me like this. I stepped away again.

"Dad, you're fucking crazy," I muttered. "You can't..."

"If I don't find you well-rested you might come home with me." This threat was real. Because he financed my apartment, I had little say over whether or not I stayed. I knew the right thing to do: take care of myself so I could convince him that everything was cool.

But there was Billie, beside another man – the rivals were everywhere and I needed to secure our love. I couldn't do the right thing and keep the one I loved. "See you tomorrow," I said, and I prayed right there, looking at the tips of the buildings, I prayed for God to restore me to sanity. I felt a gentle release, but even as I prayed for God's guidance, I stepped to Billie.

She stood with Randy, who had the long hair and beard of what Jesus might look like were he ever painted accurately. Randy had a history of hooking up with any pretty sober girl he could, so I made a point of kissing Billie on the mouth when I rejoined her. She smiled broadly, yet softly, and for good measure I kissed her ear.

"Yo, homey, what's the story?" Randy asked. I liked Randy. He was fain to speak of Melville, the Aztecs, and finger banging in the same breathless street sentence. But he needed to back away from my girl.

"Do you want to meet my father tomorrow?" I asked Billie.

Nose twitch. She would protect me from him.

"Sweet Gasoline! That would be amazing. I want to meet him," Randy answered for her. His chestnut mane churned in the wind. I found my friend's misguided eagerness endearing.

"What time?" Billie asked as she brushed a curl off my forehead. Her hands were my hands.

"Well, I have to work from five to eleven," I said, pinching the cotton of her skirt to make sure she was real. Her eyes: blue jays, camouflaged killers in a clear sky. "So maybe we could meet for brunch across the street afterward."

"Brunch at night?" Billie asked. Her narrow shoulders shuddered suddenly. "Why am I shivering? It's hot tonight." I brought an arm to her hip and held her at my side. She wrapped fingers around my hand and we melded, one body.

Her touch rushed a thought from my head, the fear of my responsibility. Of course I had to go home. I had to be at Starbucks before dawn. But I couldn't leave her side, give her to Luke, so I lingered longer. "I have to work at five in the morning tomorrow."

"And you're still here?" Randy asked, his chin askance, apparently worried. But this concern melted into admiration, a smile and a repetitive nod. "Jesus fucking Mary, you have a diesel Johnson."

"Yes he does," Billie said. The clouds around the blue jays billowed: she raised her lids. Her lips smiled smugly.

"All right!" Randy clapped, did half a dance, and grinned broadly. Having somehow never smoked, Randy's teeth were white as rolled eyes. "Good for you, John."

Dry World

"We're going to meet Brian in the Rambles. Would you like to come, Randy?" Billie asked. My stomach sank through the soles of my loafers. What the fuck was Brian up to now? Would I get cut out by the Butcher?

"Love Square? I'm game!" Randy shouted for joy. He leaped twice, his vintage high-tops giving him plenty of air.

"I need to round up some ladies, too," Billie said. "Brian has a plan." I was already churning with piss-frothy jealousy.

"Yo, honey, be selective." He waved a hairy finger in warning. "I'm not having a sober orgy with just anyone."

I did not want to let her go anywhere without me, afraid that anyone might steal what she'd stolen from me. But when I took her hand, she only squeezed it cursorily before dropping me. "Randy, I have good taste, and I'm bi." Now other women were a threat, too.

"Yes you do," Randy said, as he jumped and clicked his Nikes. "Yes you are." Billie looked at me, twitched her nose, and walked toward a bored clique of girls. Fear fought off any weariness, panic that I might lose the best lover I'd known.

"So, Chess Piece, how is she?" Randy asked me loudly.

"God," I whispered. Randy and I had explicit talks about our sex lives. Meaning I heard explicit details of Randy's sex life and he heard my whining and pining about a lack thereof. But tonight I finally had dirt for him and so I dished it without a trace of shame.

"I had the best orgasm of my life and all she did was give me a hand job."

"That girl's half-gypsy. You know she's a freak."

"Randy, stereotype." I half-laughed. After I lit a cigarette some of its smoke wafted at Randy, and he fanned his own face, smilingly annoyed. "You're a Manhattan Jew. That doesn't make you rich."

"Listen, John, I am a rich Jew. Stereotypes exist for a reason. God, I bet she's great."

"Best touch I've ever felt," I whispered through his shining hair.

"You haven't really felt mine," Randy joked and we both laughed. Randy grabbed my bony ass and I made a trumpet of it. We smiled at each other while three women looked on.

Billie had rounded up Sylvia and Opal. Both were under direction from the same sponsor not to get into any relationships, or even fool around with guys in any way. Opal had forty days off of men, Sylvia, ten months. Yet they were walking beside Randy and me toward the Seventy-second Street entrance to Central Park. There we would meet Brian.

A sense of dangerous possibility tingled the tips of my fingers as they reached for a cigarette and felt my phone vibrate. My father again.

"I'm on my way, on 96. Should be there around noon, barring traffic."

"Dad, I'm fine." I wasn't. But I believed I was, and didn't know I was lying.

"I'll believe that when I see you. I hear background noise. Are you on your way home?"

"No, I told you I'm going to Central Park."

"Do you have to work tomorrow?"

"At five am. I'm just going to stay up all night."

"You're out of control, John. I'm worried about you."

"I'm out of your control, that's what you're worried about."

"Not control, John. Loving concern."

"Dad, I'm with Billie right now. I'll talk to you later."

His voice choked into a plea. "I love you John." I couldn't obey him and keep Billie. "Please go home, please."

"I love you, too. Goodnight." I ended the call. My father was being his usual overreaching self. What could he do for me here? I was angry that he was wasting so much time on the road when it was so obvious to everyone in New York that I was fine. And why was it okay for him to thirty hours without sleep and skip his meds but that wasn't okay for me? Of course, these thoughts were dangerously misguided. I had already begun to destroy my entire life in the City and before I was through blood would flow.

Randy interrupted my reverie of justification. "Chess Piece, you got to work in the morning?"

I pumped my fists. "I'm just going to stay until then."

"Fuck entropy," Randy said, pointing at my hollow solar plexus. "You are the perpetual motion machine."

"Let's stop at that bodega," I said suddenly surging with power. My father couldn't stop me. Our Father couldn't stop me. Not when I had my credit card. "I want to buy you all gifts. You all wait outside for the surprise."

It cost only sixty dollars on my Visa to buy a case of Red Bull. I walked out of the little hole with the twenty-four cans aloft, triumphant. The women cheered. Opal literally jumped for joy, her thick blonde hair spiraling in the warm breeze. In the throes of my affliction, I not only lost track of how much I spent. I couldn't care what I spent. I lowered the case to eye level and a second cheer rose when the four saw the carton of cigarettes I'd bought as well. Over a hundred dollars gone in an instant, gone due to addictions acceptable within the strictures of recovery. Within seconds, everyone was drinking energy, everyone was smoking cigarettes. Everyone but Randy. He just carried the dry goods.

Billie and I couldn't hold hands. We each held a Red Bull and a cigarette. So I kissed her candied lips, sticky from the syrupy beverage, and she blew smoke into my mouth, and I didn't cough, I took it in, inhaling deeply, searching for the lavender beneath the pungent odors of our sober indulgence. We were a block from the park when Brian called.

"I heard your song about me and Billie," Brian said. "I can't stop listening to it."

"What song?"

"The one about killing people."

I was confused. I searched my memory and thought of the only tune with the word kill in the title. A piano ballad called "Time Always Kills."

I stopped myself from correcting his misinterpretation. These days, when I wake up and remember the murder, I regret this choice. I wince. Spasms twist my features. At the time, I thought of the song's reference to needles seeing into hearts, and figured that because Brian and Billie both had histories of IV drugs, perhaps what threw him to an erroneous conclusion. I knew words could kill, but songs seemed so harmless. I underestimated the power of melodies to catch up with me. So I said the minimum. "That's great. I'm glad you're a fan. See you soon."

Another call came in, my father. This time I ignored him. I had finished my cigarette and I needed the free hand to hold Billie's, not to listen the crazy old man's pleas for my life to be boring and safe. With all my self-knowledge, I had an idea how insane I was becoming, how unhealthy my actions were. The lack of sleep, the reckless spending, the sexual adventures: the symptoms were piling up only to be burned, and fuel me further. Of course I knew what I was doing; I just felt too good to care. From not taking drugs, I get a high that people pay big money for. Mix in some caffeine and nicotine synergy and it is enough for me to feel unstoppable and still keep my clean time. I was already shaking from my ingestion, and Billie noticed.

"Are you okay?" she asked, clasping my jittery palm between her two hands, stilling it.

"So much better than okay," I said. I realized the meaning of life and promptly forgot it. The fray was upon me. "I'm fucking great."

Sylvia and Opal walked behind us, listening to Randy rant about the existential crisis in every slasher film.

"So what's this all about?" asked Opal, her wide eyes satellite photos of Mars.

"John's going to Baptize you all tonight," Billie said. Dropped jaws of Jews while Opal and I smiled. "Not really. But we are going skinny dipping in the lake."

"Oh, that's fucking foul, John. We'll all be slime balls," said Randy. "I love it."

I cracked a second Red Bull and lit another cigarette. Billie walked ahead, talking to Randy. Bile rose in my throat, perhaps because I'd consumed nothing but sober drugs since my Indian dinner the night before.

How did he pull this off? I'd tried to organize such an outing before, but everyone recoiled. Only Randy could convince three pretty women to disrobe and frolic in patrolled, public squalor. But there was no doubt that the women were into it. If there was even a twinge of discomfort between Opal and Sylvia, it seemed to be jealousy that Randy seemed to favor Billie and not them.

Randy stepped back and away from my love and met me as a nostalgic glaze washed over his wistful eyes.

"Like old times, John." He threw an arm around me. Randy was taller than I was and I felt protected from my coming father. His matted whiskers billowed as he closed his eyes, apparently summoning another, freer time. "Before you came, John."

"Tell me a story," I said, patting my horny friend on the back. Perhaps I cared for him because I knew he wouldn't steal the girl I loved from under me. Perhaps I cared for him because I suspected his broad talk was nowhere near dangerous. I even tried to care about Randy's anecdote.

"After this meeting, two kids once had sex on the steps of the Met while a friend and I watched." Randy didn't touch Billie once. He didn't have to. She touched him. Incidental brushings of shoulders were enough for me to wish death on only him. Billie I loved too much.

Finally, what Randy said registered and I responded. "Naked?"

"What're you crazy?"

"Maybe." I finished my Red Bull and threw it as far as I could. It hit a budding tree's trunk with a clank, and I thought of spring and April's cruelty. The burning cigarette was all I had left to ameliorate the envious anger, and it was almost gone.

"Of course they were clothed." The greenery rolled overhead, a scrolling canopy blackening the deep blue sky. How could an April night be this warm? There was no way to make sense of that, or of this. "They went for maybe ten minutes. Long enough for him." Randy bobbed his eyebrows. I looked away from his face to the sway of Billie's hips. I wanted my lips back on them, for it to be just us in this synthetic wilderness. The rambles closed around us. "They were trying to be quiet about it so I supplied the moans."

Randy stooped to pick up and study a discarded condom and turned to Opal and Sylvia, who were discussing literary representations of painters. "What do you say, you fox pelts? How about a reenactment?" He produced the used latex. Opal gagged, her fair features folding into wrinkles of revulsion. Sylvia laughed, tossed her cherry wood locks, and rolled pointed eyes. Then the pair locked arms and skipped ahead to be with Billie. Randy tossed the condom into the blackened brush, sauntered after them, and, perhaps because of the crowd, Billie slipped back beside me. I wanted to swallow her hand, consume her entirely.

Dry World

Opal and Sylvia made a sandwich of Randy, linking up with each of his arms. But his posture was less assured than it had been beside my love. Then Randy bounded ahead, his oaken mane bouncing with each long stride. When far enough ahead that he could make a spectacle for all of us, he set down the good stuff. Then he ripped off his yellow tank top like a Hulkamaniac and flexed his hairy arms. Under the auburn glow of a streetlamp, he was a gilded statue in shorts. He only bowed to pick up the case of drinks and the carton of cigarettes.

Sylvia tossed hair, an endless earthy flow, and laughed. A great folk album laugh: harmonious, soothing, arresting. Opal turned back toward Billie and me. Our interlocked arms were pouring Red Bull into each others mouths. Opal smiled, mildly as the night. The verdant park seemed so small in such good company that in no time we were where we wanted to be, on the shore of the Lake. But we walked further along, away from this shore for a while, because Randy knew a more secluded spot than where we first saw the shimmer under a high crescent moon.

When we reached the rock outcropping, we stopped to undress. Randy was naked before anyone, and in the water before anyone, howling at the moon. Sylvia and Opal followed me into the water, their bared curves glistening in the pool of ectoplasm. Billie was alone on the shore. I felt enough fury to conjure some elemental of passion. Anything to save me from my father.

Billie undressed. First her skirt fell, exposing lithe thighs with a furry center. Then the T-shirt, and her breasts were like quills on the shaft of a dove's feather – round and soft yet stiff. She stood there for a while, naked, eyes locked with mine.

I sang this as I wallowed in the fetid, feculent water:

What a way to go and disappoint your father
Sometimes I don't know why I even bother
What a way to go and reassure your mother
So I say don't let go and try to love another

I felt tugs at my legs, mermaids pulling me under, and only after I surfaced, and Billie was bare on the shore, did I see Brian emerge from the forest, piercings glinting in moonlight, an ivory knife aloft. The weapon's blade glowed like a lunar sea. And while the women smiled, only Randy didn't recognize our friend. The threatening appearance of an armed stranger was enough to send Randy's hands over his shaven crotch. Like an abused child, shrill and chilling, Randy screamed.

Chapter 12

Half a Girl Plus Half a Boy

Michigan

The morning after the party, I awoke in an empty bed. The room looked exactly the same as it had when I closed heavily medicated lids. Panic overtook me. Where was Gisele? Why hadn't she slept with me? Gnawing discontent of toothy jealousy. Envy bites harder the less that's known. Within, I already knew her to be a cheat, and so threw on clothing and stomped out of O' Neill in search of reciprocity from my great unrequited reciprocal. I went straight for liquor.

Chloe Downing lived only a cigarette's walk from my place, in a narrow apartment just above a liquor store. I decided the best course of action would be to slam a half-pint of Canadian and then head up to say hi and maybe sleep with Chloe. I did just that. I was that angry at my reasons for staying clean – Gisele and my father. Keep in mind that all this was before AA, when it was seen as more of a lifestyle choice that I did not booze and not like a life and death struggle with evil in liquid form. So my return to boozing from then on came off as weirder and uncomfortable than doomed and tragic. Chloe did not even notice. Some of that may have been the distance she kept from me, though, not just physically, but in every way. We were not what we had been.

Before Gisele, I would frequently pop by Chloe's place and stay for hours of listening, to our music and to our rants. But because Gisele despised my closest female friend, I had been kept

from catching up with the subject of the novel I was publishing on
my website. That my words would have dire consequences for our
friendship had barely crossed my unsound mind. As my eager legs
bounced up the wooden stairs to a place where I'd so often staved
off loneliness, whiskey adding to their enthusiasm, I should have
known my reception would chill the air into a solid, but reason had
deserted me some months before I stood knocking on her screen
door.

I saw only a flash of her elfin face before she turned away,
unhooking the locked screen with her back to me. When I entered
she kept walking away, straight into her bedroom, until I was left in
the skinny living room. She tossed bra after bra into a pile a foot
and a half from my feet. Thoughts of her fructose breasts
unclasping drove me into a twittering frenzy as I waited for a
greeting, any acknowledgment of my existence. When it came, it
came as a shout from her bedroom, resonating through the whole
of the cramped space. When angry, Chloe's voice would leap with
the control of an experienced yodeler, and so she sang this, the
break on the third word: "How dare you bother me after last night's
debacle." A twelfth bra landed on the pile, and she stepped to face
me, her stainless silvery eyes hooking into my mouth. I was a fish
about to get gutted.

"I lost my virginity, Chloe."

She picked up a black lace bra and whipped me with it.
"Well I'm sure it was a lovely seven seconds. Hope the harpy's
happy." She threw the bra at my head.

Dry World

"I never came. I haven't yet." With my thumb and forefinger, I picked up the bra by its strap as if it were biological waste, and gently placed it back on the pile. "I get so tired of giving and giving orgasm after orgasm and getting nothing but that empty feeling after."

She softened at this, stepping over the bras and extending her narrow hand. I took it and pulled myself to my feet, but she seemed surprised by my rising. "I just wanted to shake your hand. You're the only guy I've ever heard say that. Girls, all the time. John, you really are one of us. I love you."

"I love you, too." We both had new partners, and still there was this inappropriate intensity to our amity. Chloe remained the subject of my rapt obsession. The overwrought pages I spewed into cyberspace concerned her, never Gisele. Gisele had fallen for me only as a fan of the work that her enemy had inspired, pages seething with the misdirected resentment from years of sexual frustration. Now that frustration had lessened, but the words had already been read, and there was no taking them back.
Chloe used to touch my shoulders when passing, but this time she navigated through the strait of floor between the ratty couches without even grazing me. Near the stereo hung a sheet of great quotations uttered in the apartment, about two-thirds of which I had said. "I get so tired of giving orgasm after orgasm and..." She looked to me, so I finished the repetition.

"...And getting nothing but that empty feeling after." I sat back into the generous folds of her sofa. I wanted to sink all the way into it like a foldaway mattress, disappear in the guise of something I was not, be anything other than abusive bastard who had battered her with my pen, the most cowardly sort of sword. The absurdity of my expectations sliced through me. I had come with a mind to consummate our longstanding flirtation when all she'd heard from me since I'd left town weeks before was the publicized, polluted stream of consciousness posted on my website.

"This is a song I downloaded the other day," Chloe said. "You've heard it before but I think you really need to pay attention to the words this time." It took only a single strum for me to recognize my own work. She was playing me a song I'd written about her for some reason, this:

> Don't give me Calvin College lines
> About us fated to be sad
> Why are you treating me like tapes
> Mixed by the past lovers you've had
> Don't give me sweet and low kisses
> 'Cause your aftertaste makes me mad
> Why don't you say what's really wrong?
> Is it because guys hurt you badly?

"Maybe you can see the future, John. I could swear this was written about her if I hadn't heard it a year ago." Chloe passed me again, avoiding any contact again, and fetched me a cup of coffee without even bothering to ask if I wanted it. She knew me well enough to know I'd say yes. Out the slamming screen she followed me onto the rickety, boarded fire escape, a steaming cup in each hand.

We sat on the steps and I slid her a cigarette but lit my own first. She coughed after inhaling. She only smoked around smokers and it had been almost a month since we'd done what was once a daily undertaking, unburdening our worries onto the shoulders of a loving friend. "Yellow hair, you are such a funny bear," I quoted, and she patted down my cowlick with the back of her hand.

"What is it going to take for you to realize... never mind." She shook the fine-spun gold from her eyes and laughed to herself. "You can't." She snorted, chortling. I still loved Chloe and I felt the intense desire to flee before I made some move I regretted. So I gulped coffee and set the empty mug on the wooden steps.

"Realize what?" I asked. "Realize what?"

"Nothing, it's just... words mean something, John. Think about that. I cried for days when I read the first chapter. Days."

"I didn't realize it is that good."

She flew to her feet, the boards of the wooden escape crackling as if about to snap. "Fuck you." Chloe shook more than I did, anger that had been simmering breaking into a vigorous boil. "You're the most selfish man since Jesus. Get the fuck off my porch and don't ever come back." Eyes of chrome hooks, the barbs in my heart and yanking. Going down her stairs, leaving, always felt far harder than going up. This time I knew would be the last. I didn't look back, I wanted to find Gisele and fuck the shit out of her, all while thinking of Chloe, that was my only charge, but I did stop when she called my name. "John!" I looked at cracking sidewalk under my sneakers. "I cried because it is that bad. I cried because you are that mad."

Chapter 13

What You Knew Before You Lost It

New York

Still at the Lake, I was alone with Billie. Brian's brandishing had been for show, a flaunting of his afternoon purchase of an ivory blade from a certain German vendor who peddled outside the Apple Store. My tormentor had sold Brian a weapon. But his feigned assault had been enough to murder the mood for the would-be marauder of my booty, my Billie.

Opal, Sylvia and Randy were gone. The turgid swim had lent their skin a sodden stench that each chose to lose as soon as possible. Showers were in order, so the three retired to Randy's palatial apartment near the Park. Randy had spoken openly of a group shower, but from the powerful glower on Opal's twisted lips I suspected a less interesting bathing experience was in the cards. Regardless, the three had stretched clothing over stinky skin and faded into the blackness of rustling branches past the rock outcropping, Randy stopping only to caterwaul at the diminishing moon.

Walking with a steady gale at my back: this is how every step towards mania feels. The vane points straight on till a sleepless dawn. A fatal fate there is to the weather within. The grown child pondering his reflection on the bank of a landscaped lake knew that all is vanity and a chasing of the wind, but that didn't stop even a single step. I stood from the posed repose of a nude narcissus and paced the murky muck of the shore, stimulants in either hand.

Still in the water, the daughter of an indigent Gypsy and an opulent Saxon seemed at home in the fetid foam, and in the misty distance the waif held the deceptive aspect of a naïf. Stripped of her hippie guise, diving and rising through the surface, her face aflame with shamelessness, Billie seemed cleansed of the worldly vice surely whirling in her recent past. At last, she had molted the skin of serpentine sin, and the substances once controlling her were like those clothes crinkled into rolling folds at my brown-caked feet, still there, only waited to be picked up and worn again.

Gaining the same courage that had first brought my hands to her hair only twenty-four hours before, I plunged again into the lung-punching brace of the Lake. The acceleration due to mad love brought me nearer to my dear. As I grazed her gooseflesh with a palsy-ridden palm, my thoughts were plasma, only containable by magnetic fields. There was some aligned iron attraction between us, but the fields I felt from her sped my atoms toward a super-collision where I would shatter into spiraling components. With wide eyes on the flickering skyline beyond the nearby branches, I kissed her ear. It felt cold. I felt cold.

"Let's get warm," I whispered.

"My car is three blocks west." She kissed my tremulous fingers. "Heating vents." My thumb was hers to suck. She didn't seem to understand what I was insinuating. Implied: I wanted to be inside her, to feel the inner warmth of her hot spring. But something always hung between us that made her as impenetrable as the rock outcropping we now headed for. We never did have proper sex.

"Can you give me a ride to work?" The reality of my responsibility still beat in my forebrain, even as an instinctual duality of desire fired me higher: to be insane here and to be inside her.

She rolled her eyes and brought a finger to my mouth, shutting my lips. "You're watching the sunrise with me. Let's go."

With each step toward the banks, my feet sank into the under layer of sticky mud, and had to crack out of the dankness. Our feet were shod in this mud when the last of the water fell away, so we chose to walk out without any shoes. I rolled my jeans above my calves but their lower edge still hung brown, as did patches of Billie's wide skirt.

My phone showed three missed calls, all from my father, and the time, nearly one AM. The park was about to close, and I had four hours to get downtown to open the store where I worked. I couldn't watch the sun rise with her without seriously endangering my only source of income, but to deny my Billie any whim felt like a betrayal.

So I followed her west, half a case of Red Bull and half a carton of cigarettes weighing down my arms. As if serving a child, she brought a silver-blue can to my lips and I drank. I stepped on a few extruding roots on the walk through the woods, and the knobby pavement stung my soft feet, but somehow our soles made it to the sidewalk unscathed. We passed the spectacular edifice of

Dry World

the Natural History museum barefooted and footloose, Billie stepping ahead to dance along with the wordless melody she sung to herself, muffled each time she brought a singeing cig to her lips.

Slipping higher, faster, my mind was a scattershot plotting of a thousand bright spots with no hope for a line of best fit. Random recurrences of phrases were each a point, a feeling like being fully aware of the beta wave randomness felt just before sleep. I was in deep: the grip of a complex trig function sliding me along a course I could not control.

And what of the beauty leading me on, her white fingers beckoning me to follow her along Seventy-Seventh Street? What was she if not the independent variable in the function controlling my fateful progression? No, there is no such mathematical simplicity to the course of lives. I had done just as much as her to be in the midst of a motion blur of thoughts drag racing down a dusty Michigan road, fast back to the last episode of madness two years' prior, the last interlude of passion as well. Surely their coinciding timelines were correlated, but to infer causation leaves me with too little culpability for my own moods.

Mood disorders are brainstorm fronts, and if Billie had any effect on them, it was indirect and subtle. The woman who unlocked her black Beetle that I might climb inside, this woman and the woman before her were only greenhouse gasses pumped into an incredibly complex system. I am no planet, but I have my weather within, and the effects were undeniable: I was warming; I was storming. The night's balmy calm was mood-congruent with my forming euphoria.

"I'm so high right now," I said as Billie clustered the clutter into her black backseat. Manuscripts, scribbled with marginalia; empty but in tact packs of Camel Lights; a battered guitar that looked to be from the late nineteen thirties; and one pair of paisley underwear: all this she tossed into the considerable collection of wreckage already in the rear. I climbed in as a click of the key brought a quick clang telling us to buckle, all while my clay-like feet smeared brown down on the soft stiffness of the matted upholstery. The cases of the stimulants I set beneath the messy roll of my denim. Billie reached beneath my thighs to grab another can, her hands now shaking as mine always shook, and the brush of her wrist against me winced the winch between my legs. As she pulled the bubbly black car out of its tight-fit spot with quick strokes of the reeling wheel, I had to ask what she already grasped. "Where are we going?"

"Your place, of course." The bright brocade of Broadway lights scrolled by like an unwrapping tapestry. The intricate weave of Times Square felt like the fabric of my mind. The synthetic city was the loom that had crafted my rapture and captured me in its interwoven manifestation of madness.

Had Billie only known the irreverent reverie swirling beneath the curls she stroked, as her palsied palm slipped into a gentle grip of my skulls base, as if cradling the weak neck of a newborn. But she didn't even know the nature of my malady, how bad I already had it. I couldn't tell her straight away, not with my thoughts so frayed that I felt my very cells might unravel and leave me as little more than a pile of protoplasm in her car. So I played her this, and said, "Listen. Every word is true."

Dry World

Took away my guitar today
Said I'd hang myself on the strings
Hate to admit thought I know it
I'm a part of material things
I checked in to the loony bin
To be forgiven for the sin
Of believing she was God
She perfect, my existence flawed
Lost myself in the love for one
I placed higher than the sun
And worshipped like an Egyptian
From my earthly position
Did you ever have the choice to choose?
Did you ever find a mind to lose?

"When did you write that?" Billie asked, switching off the stereo after the last of the music faded.

"During my last episode." I lit a cigarette, took a long, dramatic drag, and let the smoke flow from my lips for long enough to draw her eyes from the road. We were stopped at a light, and I met her wary gaze as the light switched. "I'm crazy, Billie. And I'm mad right now." A chorus of horns rose behind us before she looked back to the road and accelerated down the broad diagonal.

"Some one once raped me during his psychotic episode," Billie said, flatly, as if she were a reporter reading a horrendous story. Her hands nowhere near me, her eyes frightfully flat. I looked into my translucent reflection in the passenger window and I could see my father in my face, the father who was in his station wagon, probably entering the foothills of western Pennsylvania. "Are you psychotic now?" she asked, a killing shrillness to the plea.

"Two years ago. It's like the climate, Billie. My seasons in the brain. A menstrual cycle of the heart. That time of the year. The weather within."

"Call your brother. Make sure he's home." And as if cued to our conversation, George came up on the phone's display. A text message: come homey.

We were downtown by then, heading east down Spring Street. We passed the store where I was supposed to be in a very short time, we passed the late night lounge crowd of smoking revelers, we passed it all in silence until we turned up Elizabeth. Her car slowed, and I realized she wasn't parking, she was dropping me off, this was it, she was gone, we were finished: so fast did my thoughts progress to our undoing.

"George is home?" Billie asked. Her face tentative, spent.

I nodded.

"You need to be with your family now."

I went for lips but got her cheek. Unspeakable disappointment in the peachy texture of her face, the taste like that of a priceless wine opened only to find fine vinegar. Thoughts of getting drunk arose and passed away.

"Take care of yourself, John." A look of pithy pity hit me, as if she'd shared a pitcher of beer with a cirrhosis sufferer.

Dry World

I stepped out of her car, the carton and the case in my vibrating hands, and she had to shut the door behind me. I abandoned all hope before her brake light circles shrunk down the narrow, leafy stretch of Elizabeth Street.

Chapter 14

Give Up the Nightlife

Michigan

Gisele licked her miniature finger to turn a gilded page of my boyhood Bible. She sat curled in a front porch couch of O' Neill, reading the good book. Her thick auburn hair hung in damp clumps, and one thin chunk split her wide eyes at the thin bridge of her nose. In the muted shade beneath the portico, she effused an innocence I knew to be nonsense. She didn't look up from her page until I sidled into the corduroy cushion beside her.

"Ecclesiastes, naturally," she said. "All is Vanity." Nose twitch.

"The new translation: everything is meaningless."

"It just isn't as poetic that way. Are you drunk?" Her lids squinted and the chunk shook free from her face.

"I was sure you'd be reading the Song of Solomon."

"Is that your idea of a pick up line?" Her eyes went back to the text.

I clenched her wet hair. "Don't you ever use a blow drier?"

She sniffed my wet pit. "Don't you ever take a shower?"

"At least I slept," I said. "Where did you go?"

She got sarcastic. "It must be so hard for you to sleep on all those drugs." Her sneer softened, and a faraway look passed over her eyes before she closed them and said, "I try to wake you late and give up every time. If you had any idea how much sex you're missing, you'd probably kill yourself." A hit between my hazel eyes. Truth was the only counterpunch I needed.

"I just got back from Chloe's."

"I just got back from Tom's." I stood and lit a cigarette. She had spent the night with her ex while we were living together. I wanted to believe they had only spoken of old times, shared their sixteen years of common history in conversation. I was already sure she would say that was all that happened, and I would have no choice but to believe her. So I didn't bother following up on her late night excursion.

Instead I told her how much whiskey was in me, then exhaled a cloud that hung like an apparition in the stagnant spring air. I wanted to run back to Chloe's arms, feel the last hug that she gave me a few days before Gisele metastasized in my stuttering heart, before I posted enraging pages, functional images of this cancer at work.

"Big difference, John." She arched her back, apparent anger aligning her spine. The rise of her perched chest inflamed my irate desire. I wanted to take her there, with a crowd from the house cheering me on. But I didn't, I only turned away and faced the fluttering foliage above the grass-cracked sidewalk. "Chloe was never your girl. Tom and I were together for three years."

"How many novels have you written about Tom?" It occurred to me then, for the first time, the idea that would invite her to destroy herself – I considered writing the confidential, twisted history of my current lover into my own garbled memoir. Parrying with the pen felt like the solution to the plague of anger festering in my four chambers. A satisfied smile split my thick lips, and I took a pull off my smoke. The cancer would spread from my heart to my art, and there were even fewer inhibitions to slow me than there had been an hour earlier.

I heard Gisele slam the book shut, and turned around. "I couldn't get next Saturday off."

"Gisele, that's Paul's wedding day." I brought long fingers across my mouth, and tapped the tip of my narrow nose. With the slurring gesture I dropped my cigarette and had to stoop to retrieve it. She didn't kick me while I was down.

"I'm just working half a shift. So I can drive in for the reception."

"It's two hours away. That won't work." I stood, the sodden cigarette back between my lips. Gray flecks of it tipped onto my white shirt, and as I blew them off she set the book aside. Gisele stood then and stepped across the dingy planks, her flats clacking until her arms were around me, her fresh lavender fragrance a scent so intense I couldn't even smell my smoke.

"It'll have to." I almost acquiesced, but the part of me she never held rebelled, as I thought of phrases to describe her violent childhood. I was like that: I could taste revenge even as I smelled ardor and booze. In my mind, she had surely fucked Tom, as surely as I was wasted in the morning. I had left for less than an hour and found her atoning for guilt by browsing my Bible. Vengeance would be mine. I would repay. Thus I plotted even as I plead.

"At least you have seven days to find someone to cover your shift."

"Why did you go see Chloe?" A whisper, hot breath on my ear, moisture like a sodden summer wind. The answer came to me then, an answer that would enrage her in the coming days, an answer I was too sane to say. I would always care for Chloe: she had been less a cancer and more a cure, taking care of me through troubled times. Empty glasses of milk we'd shared split memory's light into a spectrum. I had hoped she would be radiant therapy for the disordered growth of my love.

But I couldn't answer that, so I asked, "Why did you go see Tom?"

"I got really sick last night. He took care of me." And there it was: my answer. We had caregivers before we were with each other: mine was Chloe, only a friend; hers was Tom, more than that. "You never answered my question."

"Was it explosive diarrhea?" I asked. She laughed, and some of the tautness slipped from the knot in her taut backbone.

"Sick from whiskey."

"I wouldn't know anything about that." I winked, her nose twitched, and I put a hand on each of her slight shoulders and pulled back, meeting her wary, weary gaze. Blue-gold blinked, its aspect hardening like a sterile scalpel.

"I tried to wake you up, tried for an hour, but you were down on those fucking drugs."

"So you called Tom?" My disease was taking her from me. If I hadn't been under such severe treatment, I might have been present for her when she needed me. I might have kept her from the arms of her former lover. I might still be sober. Now my hands were shaking so badly that she must have felt as if I were shaking her. "Why didn't you just ask someone in the house?"

"Tom saved my life, John. Last time I wanted to die he held me back." And there it was, a declaration I should taken with greater gravity. Instead, I thought only of myself, my health, how all this was wracking my wreck of a head with anxious stress. "I need him."

Paul approached from the sidewalk. If he had been Tom, I might have screamed at him. But I was scared of my brother, his imposing presence looming inches higher than my tall frame. My mind was nowhere near him, though, it was on those last three words out of Gisele's fat lips.

"As a friend, of course," she added after a pause. Far too long I waited for the words. I'd seen the future in a flash. She wasn't the protector I thought she was. She needed a protector of her own, anyone other than me. We were wholly halves that could never add up. She would never make the scene in the dry world dream. And here was Paul, from whom I needed protection in those childhood days of abuse, present to torment me again.

"Are you ready for Roosevelt tomorrow?" my brother asked. He looked like a doctor insuring his partner in a procedure would be competent.

"What?" I had no idea he was planning on going home. He had not visited my parents since he'd moved to Ann Arbor to work construction and score college girls. My only thought was that George got to him, made him consider showing up for his beloved mother. "I'm going to meet Gisele's mom." I wasn't that excited about this prospect, as Gisele had briefed me with horror stories of physical and mental abuse from her single parent.

"Un-fucking-acceptable, John. It's Mother's Day. If I'm going home, you're sure as hell coming with me." As I tossed aside my cigarette he brought two fingers to his lips and I fished out one for him. I was such an addict that I couldn't light his without lighting another of my own. "What did you get her?"

"I hadn't even thought about it." I felt a twinge of guilt in my throat, having been so consumed with my first relationship that I'd forgotten about filial piety. The year before, when I had no one, I'd written her a song and sent her flowers. Now I was so wrapped up in the sinews of a metastasizing lust and I'd just forgotten.

"Typical," Paul said. "You know how Hallmark she can be. Are you trying to break her heart?"

"What about Dad?" I thought of him facing my father across a dinner table, and Gisele there. Perhaps it was all just a rehearsal for the rehearsal dinner that coming Friday.

"I bought Mom this nice video camera," Paul said.

"With what?"

"I was in Detroit getting... I was in Detroit and this guy had a nice selection in his trunk. Cheap, too."

"John's coming with me." Gisele stepped between Paul and me. She put out a hand to ward off my brother and he mistook this for a grasp for a pass of this cigarette. She waved him off and continued. "I need backup facing my mom."

"If she's such a bitch, just come with us."

"I will." Gisele didn't need much of an excuse to avoid her mother. Her response was instant relief, the yardstick of her spine disappearing. "Let's caravan."

Paul nodded and headed off, probably to a bar. But before he left the portico, he stopped and leaned on a column, his skin tanned and leathery against its bright white. "What were you guys fighting about anyway?"

Dry World

I sang a line of mine: She wouldn't give up the night life, and be my wife.

"Save the songs for the suckers," Paul said, and clomped down the seven stairs into the wildly overgrown lawn. "And John," he added, "Switch to vodka. Whiskey smells every time."

Chapter 15

Between Half-Embraces

New York

My mood was fucked as I climbed the stairs to my second floor walkup, the inverse of what it had been with Billie behind me just one day before. Each step up was like walking on the surface of a planet twice as massive as earth. The clear lyricism of my mad romance had crashed down around me, accelerated due to the gravity of my actions. Thoughts that were once lighter than air felt denser than lead, but still flew with the velocity of bullets through a brain. I had gone insane and in a matter of hours I would have to face my father. I reached the landing with only a distant awareness that it might be George who needed consolation.

The cabin still smelled faintly of disinfectant, so I lit a cigarette to replace one stench with another. My brother whirled his mop around when I entered, but didn't stand, only fixed his God-frightened eyes on my slouching frame. The weight of forty-plus hours awake was breaking over my back, and I still had many to go before I could give in to sleep. If I went down then, I would miss work, I might even miss lunch with my father. No, there was no way I could sleep as I was, and yet every cell in my weary body felt spent of energy.

"You look cashed," George said. I slid off my scratched loafers and stepped past the lidless vigil of Grandpa Rook's deer, over bearskin, to the davenport.

Dry World

There, sliding into its red and black flannel folds, I said, "I feel like a bouncing check."

George offered me a sip of water and I gulped his whole glass. I had lost track of the number of energy drinks I'd downed and I was as dehydrated as anyone with a hangover. He new the problem without a word from me.

"Who is she?" A faucet turned as George refilled his glass with tap water. He had met Billie the night before but now it seemed he had only a hazy recollection of his drunken introduction.

"A program girl."

The faucet turned again as he filled a second glass. "Convalescing but coalescing?"

"Better than just sick."

"True." He returned to the davenport and passed me a glass of water.

"I need you to stay up with me until I go into work."

"Will do, sir."

I brought my smoking hand to my forehead and smoothed its furrows. "I think it's over."

"Already?"

"She found out I'm mentally ill." My cigarette was finished. I was finished. I pinched out its tip with a singe of my calloused fingers and dropped the butt onto the shiny hardwood.

"So? Who isn't these days."

"She has a bad, bad history with guys like that."

"Are you psychotic?"

"I'm something."

George took a long drink of water. He swallowed hard, took another drink, and swallowed hard again. "You should probably sleep then."

"If I crash now I won't make it in to work."

"John, you are more important than the coffee machine." We had the same eyes, Almost green and very weary from birth.

I looked out at the leafy folds of the budding trees lining the street below. If I focused on branches they would go limp and then tie themselves into nooses. Soon enough there was no tree; there was only a bloom with gallows as petals. Death coming to life. "I want to die, George."

"This girl, I'm guessing."

"Her name is Billie."

"Might as well be Gisele."

I walked over to the window and thought about jumping out. Headfirst and I might have a chance at not having a chance, but the angle would have to be just right. I saw a pretty head split open, a red slit, and gray shit oozing onto concrete. This was swept away by the swipe of a brown cardinal's wing. "I don't want to talk about her."

"Just don't start writing about Billie. Or if you do, don't publish on the Internet. Or if you do don't tell all her secrets. Because…"

"George, she's not going to kill herself."

"John, you said the same thing about…"

The trees were whispering through the panes, a thousand Giseles telling me to fell myself. Anger was the only emotion I could manage. "Enough!" I kicked the bear rug in the eye. "Shut the fuck up and go make me some coffee."

"Dad's going to be pissed when he smells the smoke in here."

I tipped ash onto the davenport and said, "Dad can suck his own dick."

"Take your meds, John. Please." Thoughts branched, and branched again, and again, and at the end of each dendrite was the same hanging rope, choking me. I was not so lucky as to have my neck break. "Call in sick. You're not well."

I picked up the phone and dialed my manager. "Hi, Phil, this is John Rook. I'm not going to be in to work tomorrow morning, in three hours, whatever, because I've had a complete nervous breakdown. Thanks. Have a good life."

George laughed. I crouched to make up with Lucius, petting his black and tan head. "Okay," George ordered, "Now call Dad. He's been bugging me all night."

I picked up the phone and dialed my father. "Hi Dad this is John. I'm home now. How much medication should I take to shake this?"

"How are you doing?" he asked, to which I only responded with silence. "That well. Take a double dose. I'll be there when you wake."

I hung up on him. He called back but I turned the phone off. I uncoiled my arm from around Lucius, let go of my pet carpet. "I'm going to bed."

Drugs swallowed, I wallowed in sweaty sheets for an hour before the downers broke through all the uppers in my system. While I was rolling between wakefulness and sleep, I heard George singing and playing guitar through the shared wall between our bedrooms. It was a song I wrote, which somehow made me sadder still:

Dry World

When my beagle died in the arms I waste
And my brother cried as a dug a place
For the dog to lie with a bitter face
In our tears we cried but could not embrace

Then at last, I shifted into a dream of a sandy planet.

The second moon rose yellow among the alien stars, full like the first already high above the desert waves. A steady flow of airborne grains lightly pelted my legs bellow the calf. The night was warm, almost hot, and sand clung to the sweat under my linen suit. Each step squeaked a collapsing crater into the ridge of the dune. Dunes stretched to the horizon, not a rock or a ridge anywhere in sight.

A tug at my billowing robe. I looked behind me, and there stood the black-veiled woman. The light of the moons brightened her eyes, four sparkles. They hung only a few inches below my line of sight; she was tall. I reached to lift the veil, and she caught my grasp with both of her hands, and held my palm, stroked my knuckles. Undaunted, I persisted. I lifted the veil.

Her face was my face, but feminized: smooth where I had whiskers, smaller to fit her body, hair long and straight where mine was short and curly. Yet the resemblance was beyond even that of some lost sister. She looked just like me and I had never been more aroused.

I smiled at her and she smiled at me, simultaneously. I shook my head and she shook her head in time with mine. I curled my upper lip, and again her expression mirrored mine. Each changed happened as mine happened.

Dylan James Brock

Then she took over. I felt her unsheathe an ivory knife
from beneath her black robe and I did the same, finding one
hanging inside my linen blazer. I felt her point the knife at her heart
and I did the same, its tip indenting the breast of my cotton shirt. I
felt her end her life and I did the same, ending the dream.

Chapter 16

Mother Gave Two Magnets

Michigan

We three sat on the patio behind my home: Mary Rook, my lover, and I. My older brother and father were off watching Detroit basketball together. My younger brother had wandered down the shore in search of the fly lord flicker of children around a fire. I sat there with lines from a song of mine looping in my head:

> As a child mother gave me two magnets
> To show me how to attract and repel
> Playing I thought I could find the distance
> Where fields floated apples that never fell
> I have yet to achieve levitation
> These days I'd settle just for levity
> I no longer believe if I'm patient
> I'll balance our charged similarities

While Gisele sipped a carafe of sun-blackened tea, its cubes jangled a discordant harmony with the distant clink of wind chimes. Off the Lake, the evening breeze billowed along dune blades, but not the short-cropped lawn. The scent of just-clipped grass wafted from this green carpet. My right stroked the velveteen ears of the lion hound, until, irritated, she flopped them like an organic helicopter. My left kept swirling the glass it held, neat whiskey swirling slower than water would have. Over the stretched arms of a flat water horizon, green and red lights of a prop plane passed the auburn glow of Mars, shining in that summer of 2003 brighter than it had in decades.

"Thirty years ago I fell for your father," my mother said, as she fingered a ring on her elegant digits. "We were engaged after three weeks." Mary Rook had beatifically beautiful eyes, weary from years of sympathetic suffering. They hung over a gently rolling Roman nose, framed by sienna hair that hung past her shoulders. Her arms were deeply tanned, flecked with constellations of flat moles, and it was only by studying her neck and hands that one could discern her age.

"Why do you wear the ring on your right hand?" Gisele asked. She liked my mother, I could tell, but then again I have yet to meet anyone who disliked Mary Rook.

"This is what Jack gave me." My mother held up her left hand. Its tendons ran in ridges along suede shoe wrinkles. On her left finger: an unimpressive strip of hard gold around a diamond bit. "All he could afford as a musician. He wasn't a doctor till I got a hold of him."

"What's that, then?" Gisele asked, pointing at my mother's other ring finger. There, a Jameson family heirloom: platinum filigree around a two-carat stone.

"My grandmother invented frozen dinners. It was hers." Her eyes collected the night light into a regal, distant stare, something like a painting of a benevolent monarch.

"May I?" Gisele reached for the ring, avarice in her nimbus eyes. While she held it up to the light cast across the wide backyard, my mother looked to me.

"Paul inherited the ring Jill wears from Grandma Rook, so John..."

"Mom!" I chided, feeling nervous at how forward her implication was.

"John, it's okay. I'm just keeping this ring until John gets engaged. We have heirlooms for each of the boys."

"I've never seen a ring like this," Gisele said softly, as if talking to herself.

"You should see the ring she wears for George," I said. "A whole village of South Africans got hobbled for that one."

Gisele laughed, but my mother took a long sip of red wine, smacked her thinning lips, and took another sip. "If you could live anywhere," my mother asked, "where would you go?"

"New York," I said, but she wasn't asking me. Gisele screwed her broad lips into a disgusted smirk. She had never been to my favorite city and had no desire to remedy that.

"I'm from California originally," Gisele said, pride in her wide set eyes. Nothing above her mouth was lit. A blossoming crab apple tree cast shade across the top half of her face. Its petals fluttered down in the zephyr off the water: spring snowflakes. Only two weeks before there had been an ice storm. Gisele wanted to get somewhere without winter. "I'm moving to Marin County as soon as I can."

"Vermont. That's where I need to be," my mother said. She had a bad habit of crying when drunk. The crab apple tree shaded her face as well, but I could tell her tears from years of studying her face. She pinched the bridge of her arching nose and said, "A horse farm near Lake Champlain. John's going to buy it for me when he's rich and famous."

Gisele laughed, dismissing such an absurd possibility.

"Quiet, you," I said to Gisele, waving her off with a flail of my spidery hand. "You only lived in California till you were three. You're from Michigan like the rest of us."

"I'm from Willamette," my mother said, looking southwest over the black stretch of night waves, as if there were lights of invisible cities to be seen past the horizon.

"Chicago?" asked Gisele.

"North Shore," said my mother.

"Only the richest spot in the Midwest," I said.

"I thought I was from there," Gisele said. She liked to introduce herself as the poorest girl in Bloomfield Hills, a wealthy suburb of Detroit.

"New money," my mother said, flat voiced, as if expressing emotion about such people would be beneath her. "I spent my senior year of high school there. A nightmare. There's really nothing akin to the Gold Coast in Michigan."

149

"I know what you mean. We must've graduated from the same school," Gisele said. "I never did adjust after California."

"After infancy?" I laughed and stroked her hand. She pulled it away and reached for her tea. "You moved at three," I said.

"It is where I was born," she said.

"I know what you mean," my mother said. She had lived in Roosevelt all my life and yet she still said she was from Illinois. "If I hadn't moved to Michigan, I would have never met Jack and I wouldn't be stuck in Roosevelt."

"I'm falling in love with Roosevelt," Gisele said.

"You're falling in love with John," my mother corrected. "Just don't mistake that for a love of where he is. You meet a charmer from his little city, he sucks you down his toilet, and you call it refreshing. Look what I got."

"The most beautiful house I've ever seen?" Gisele said. Money went much further in Roosevelt than where either of these women was from. My parents could afford lakeside acreage and a palace only because of the absurdly depressed real estate market. We had already popped all the bubbles in Michigan.

"I would give up anything to give up this." She looked at me and smiled weakly. "Anything except my family, of course."

"I want to move here," Gisele said. "John and I could rent a house for the price of a room in Ann Arbor."

"Come only until you have enough to move far, far away," my mother said.

"New York," I said.

"Marin," Gisele said. She shook her head and brought a hand over her eyes. She gulped the rest of her sun tea, and my mother gulped the rest of her Chianti.

"Well, good night. I have to hold babies for money in the morning."

"I'm falling in love with Roosevelt, too," I said to Gisele.

"John, you listen to me." My mother touched me as she spoke, and she only touched me when what she said was very important. She set her suede hand on my wrist and clenched. "You must get out. Must. Get out so I can get out. This is a great place to be when you're a kid, but, as an adult, living here is worse than dying." She whirled around, her hair whipping like the train of a bride in a gale.

My mother was still near when Gisele spoke ill of her at an inappropriate volume. "Now I see why you're a drama queen, John."

When my mother stopped and turned back to face my lover, I couldn't bear the look of hurt on her face. So I covered my eyes, and only heard her laugh nervously. My mother said, "I am the drama queen. John's just the second prince."

Dry World

"Narcissism is a family disease," I said to Gisele, as my mother disappeared behind the slam of a French door. "It's all about us."

Chapter 17

Equal in Misery

New York

We three sat in a diner booth: my father, my brother, and I. With the pale green fluorescent lighting and the one plate glass window up front, there was no way to tell that it was just after noon inside. My brown spotted mug was as empty as I felt and had my same low chances of ever feeling full again. Medication shakes fluttered my fingers like the wings on the fly buzzing around my plate of dryly scrambled eggs. I ate the terrible food in chunks so wide that yellow clumps fell onto my black hooded sweatshirt. I didn't mind. There were already clusters of gray stains from ash flecks rubbed into the fabric. With my sleeve I wiped my mouth, a mouth that hung slack as a yokel's.

Dad had been talking quickly, wildly, happily with my studious brother. George had a four point after his first semester of college and Jack couldn't hide his vicarious satisfaction. Paul and I were such worthless fuck ups and financial drains, but apparently the parents got it right on the third try. I looked at the way my father looked at George, but I couldn't feel enough to be envious. All I could manage was relief that perhaps I wouldn't have to do as well anymore now that my father had a real hope. Their chatter couldn't register in my prairie-sparse brain, wide and void as a grazing range for starving cattle. I ate a delicious chunk of gristle from the steak on my bloody plate, wondering if Brian's ivory knife could saw metal as well as meat. My father made the crack he always made when we ate together: "You always eat your food one dish at time. First all the eggs, then all the steak, then all the potatoes, then all the toast. It's so odd."

Though my mouth was empty, I only grunted in response. An insanely high dose of Zyprexa, 50 milligrams, had turned off the spigot on my stream of consciousness. No words formed in my head, and those I said came in inaudible mutterings. It was the strangest thing: they sounded bell clear to me, but to others, they were all but babble. So I said little when under the brain cloud, and people sometimes mistook this for wizened pensiveness, which it wasn't. I couldn't pay attention to anything for long enough to be pensive. About the only productive things I did well when thus drugged was play guitar and eat, and I was sloppy when doing even those. The home fries were not spiced, only salted, but I plowed through them anyway. I remembered eating at this place when I first moved to New York a year before and finding it delicious. Now it tasted so bland that only my father seemed to be enjoying his meal.

"Zyprexa works fast," my father said, diagnosing my side effects.

I nodded and excused myself for a cigarette. If I could feel anything, I might have been angry at his intervention, but as I was I could only manage passive aggression. My father hated when I smoked and every time I lit up it was a fuck you to him.

Jack looked at home on the squeaky vinyl seats. His button down shirt had been ironed by my mother, but its print was hopelessly out of place – trout and tied flies. The jeans were too pale, too baggy, and his shoes were the frumpy yellowing sneakers of a weekender who just couldn't give a shit. I had caught him unaware, at home on a Saturday and he must have driven in what he'd been in at the time of the first call.

Not that I was in a position to judge. I had thrown on soiled jeans and soiled socks, and the sweatshirt looked like a black cat rolling in a litter box. I didn't look out of place on Lafayette Street. I just looked like the useless piece of transient trash I was. I no longer felt mixed. I no longer felt.

What thoughts I had were utterly dejecting. Billie wanted nothing to do with me because I reminded her of her rapist. I would never be with her even if I were with her again. And only when I had all the hope of the hell-bound did I remember where I would see her, with someone else: the sober prom. It was only in a few days, and I already had a date, I was going with a friend, Opal. She would probably go home with some other guy just as Billie would likely do. There was no chance for me to be with anyone.

Just at the point when the crawling thoughts of a depressive reverie collapsed, exhausted, it occurred to me that I hadn't come to New York City to get girls. I had come because of the opportunity my father would surely remind me of in a moment. I was working for a great man. The day before I had sat with him just outside this same diner, only a few steps from where I was puffing on my cigarette then.

Just the thought of my boss drew my eyes to the sky and take notes on the weather. It was cloudy, the air wet and threatening to condense into droplets at any moment. Still, the sky was neither darkening nor lightening. Instead it stayed the same matte wall of gray, looking as though the whole ceiling of the city was one thick puff of cigarette smoke.

The air near the ceiling of a particularly crowded bar came to mind, one like Roger's hangout. There the laws of the city had somehow been circumvented. Those were the only bars Roger would meet at – he insisted that a sober man like himself had no reason to be in a place that did not let him indulge as it let others indulge. He went so far as to turn down readings where alcohol would be served. He was that attached to his cherry cigarillos and my light cigarettes.

I was done smoking, and had even scrawled a page of notes and observations in the Elizabeth Street journal. Unfortunately, this meant there was no longer any excuse to avoid the family for the time being. I coughed, I inhaled deeply, I coughed again, and I plunged back into the diner. My brother and father sat quietly, sipping coffee, obviously waiting for me. We all had the same eyes – hazel, spaced wide, lashed with natural liner, under thick mocha brows. The difference – theirs were alert, astute, while memory of medicated reflections told me mine were as lifeless as those of a rigid corpse. I no longer wanted to die, but only because I no longer wanted anything except to eat and be left alone. I would have no such luck with an imperialistic parent across from me. It was enough for me to wish there were isolationist tax positions I could take to keep my parents out the way a country could do the same to all those around it. All I wanted was to hop in a cab to Billie's apartment afterward, but there was this old man to deal with. And I wasn't about to get the conversation off to a start with my mumbling cadence, so I sighed and threw up my hands and Jack began his inquisition.

"How's Roger?" my father asked.

"Fine, I guess. I'm not his doctor," I said, leaning my elbow onto the give of the seat, as if I were about to doze off right there.

"I know that, John," he said, grasping the air as if he could wring water out of its unconditioned humidity. "What I mean is, how's the work for him going?"

"Fine."

"What are you researching now?"

"Parricide."

George laughed at this for some reason I couldn't process.

"Murdering your father?" asked my father.

"That's patricide," I said.

"Oh, so when you murder both your parents," my father said.

"Like that guy by our house," George said. "Only he took out the dog, too. Is there good psychiatric literature on canicide?" He looked to me for a chuckle of understanding but I could only smile.

"I'm confused," my father said.

"Canicide. The murder of dogs," George said as he raised an eyebrow.

"Not much on just parricide," I said.

"Why on earth would you want to know about parricide?" My father asked as he shook his enormous head. My head was huge too, but his hung over a small body and looked out of place there. He continued: "It's so awful I can't imagine it would interest anyone."

"Dad, there's obviously a direct proportion between the awful and the interesting," George said as he rolled eyes up and shook his head.

Only then did I notice the waitress had refilled my coffee while I'd been outside. I was that out of it. I sipped it, found it cold, and gulped it anyway. I needed all I could get to pry myself out of my phlegmatic apathy.

"So how much work did you do for Roger last week?"

"About twenty hours," I lied. I had done the minimum: ten.

"John, I'm not paying for you to be here so you can make that kind of slacker effort. You know how many hours I worked last week?"

I shook my head and brought my hands over my eyes to hide from him.

"Dad works one-hundred sixty-eight hours a week," George said. "Except during those damn time changes."

"Actually I worked eighty-four hours, clocked. You know why?"

"Because you're awesome?" answered George.

"No, because I have two boys in the most expensive city in the world."

"Tokyo is worse," George said.

"How many hours are you supposed to do for Roger?" asked Jack.

"Ten," I said.

"And how many hours do you work at Starbucks?"

"Twenty or thirty."

"So you did forty hours of work last week?"

I nodded.

"That's not going to cut it in your town."

"I studied fifty hours last week," George said. He looked like he belonged where he was: NYU in 2005. The mod ray bans indoors certainly helped. "And I went to all seventeen hours of class."

"So you did sixty-seven hours of work last week?"

"Oh, at least," George said. He took off the glasses to look my father in the eyes with a nod. He wasn't lying, either. He had my father's work ethic. I had my mother's.

Had I been cognizant, I might have fired facts at the old man. I couldn't argue with him, as sedated as I was, so I said all I could. "I'm sick."

"I know, John. It must be hard for you. I can only imagine." I didn't know how to respond to this. He was crazy and he didn't take his meds. Why couldn't I function? Delayed anger registered, like a thunder lizard reflex, so I took out a cigarette, lit it, and tipped it into his water. This was against the law, of course, smoking inside a diner. The wait staff approached to chide me, but I hadn't done it to be insolent. I was just so out of it that I didn't care where I was. In one slick move, George slipped an arm around my father and bribed the server with a ten-dollar bill, so she would leave me be. She snatched it and scurried away. It was the kind of place where people took such bribes, even small ones, and it was empty anyway.

"You used to be like us, John. Remember, Dad, before you drugged him? John was a fucking dynamo." He was trying to cheer me up, I knew, but he was only making me feel worse the longer he went on. "You studied fifty hours a week in Junior High, for God's sake. Everyone thought, doctor, lawyer, president, who knew? Big things were in store for John Rook. And now..."

"Now I'm sick," I said and took a long drag. My dad wasn't registering the lawbreaking. You could smoke in Michigan diners back then.

"Maybe you can do a little more for Roger this week." I honestly don't know that he understood I was breaking the law as we spoke. "Thirty hours? Forty? The more you do for him the more he'll do for you."

"Quid pro quo," George said. "This town is all about who you know and who you help."

"You've won half the battle, George. You know Roger Abbey."

"I help him," I said, as let smoke flow from my mouth like fire spreading under a heavy door.

"He buys John records," George said. "That's how he pays him."

"I didn't know that," my father said. The scowl was gone. The mention of music made him smile for the first time since he'd arrived. "You never told me that. What does he buy you?"

"John has every album by the Beatles now, and all the good Lennon solo stuff. What was the last one? Plastic Ono Band?"

"Double Fantasy," I said.

"It's too bad you don't have any Paul McCartney," my father said seriously. "His solo stuff is so good."

George laughed but our father ignored him.

"I can't do this on this," I said before taking a long drag.

"What?" my father asked. "Oh, you mean the dose. You can't work eighty-four hours like me on fifty of Zyprexa, and I wouldn't expect you too. But you can do more, John. You can always do more."

"If I live," I said. After another pull on the smoke, my eyes watered, but I attributed to the cloud building around me.

"John, you've made it through worse," my father said. "It's this girl, isn't it?"

"I don't want to talk about it," I said, as I wiped my eyes with my smoking hand and singed a hanging lock of my hair.

"What's her name?" my dad asked.

I stamped out my butt. "I don't want to talk about it."

"Did something already happen?" asked my dad.

"She knows I'm sick," I said, and lay down across the booth, looking up at the ceiling, until my heavy eyes gave in to their weight and closed.

"That must be scary for her," my father said. "Well, give her time. It's not easy to be with you, John. When are you going to see her again?"

"Thursday." I could feel the weight of death's silent steps on rickety floorboards. Stealthily, it was approaching again, to take someone close to me again, as it had taken someone in Michigan. The ivory knife would fall. Brian. I had to meet him at one, outside the Broadway-Lafayette station. We were supposed to review AA literature together. My mind was on the near future but my father wouldn't give up on his entreaties into my love life.

"Do you guys have a date then?"

"There's this thing," I said, rising to sit upright again. "She'll be there."

"So you made plans?"

I sighed from frustration. "No." I took out another cigarette but didn't light it.

"John, you have to take charge. I know things are hard for you. Especially since Jezebel..."

"Gisele," George and I both said at once.

"...since Jessie did what she did, you have a hard time reaching out."

"It's always been hard," I said.

"Not everyone meets their wife at twenty-one," George said, his eyes on my father.

"Yes, but after the accident John hasn't had anything and…"

"Gisele did it on purpose," I corrected him, and rose to my feet. He was pushing into painful regions, where pinched nerves still throbbed.

"Be that as it may, we don't know for sure do we? Impossible to say."

"I was there. I know."

"So what do you guys want to do today? I was thinking we could go see Madame X. It's always been my favorite painting."

"I have to go," I said, backing away, my hands up as if they were mugging me.

"Okay. Where?" my father asked.

"I have to meet someone," I said over my shoulder, after I turned.

"Okay. Who?"

"Goodbye," I said and walked out without looking back.

My father called me as soon as I was outside and I answered. "George and I will go to the Met, then. And we'll meet up for dinner. Where do you want to go? I was thinking that pizza place, the first one. At seven."

"Fine," I said and hung up. And as I passed the inert brunching crowds sipping mimosas, I started to sing loudly, and it was enough to draw the eyes of onlookers:

> You want to die
> I want to die
> We have so much in common
> If we could lie
> And never lie
> I'd be more than your shaman
> You want a jerk
> I want a jerk
> Yet we're nice to each other
> If we weren't hurting
> To be hurt
> I'd be more than your brother
> Soviet Union
> That's all we'll ever be
> Soviet Union
> Equal is misery

I decided to show my father what a work ethic could be, how much I could do if I ceased sleep, and knew that I wouldn't be taking my medication again any time soon.

Chapter 18

The Sky Opened Up

Michigan

The stars were fried country bright the night Paul met the Devil. When my brothers and I got home, Gisele and I joined them for a fire on the beach. Like a forest fire, the moon shone through the black ridge of trees lining the dune's lip. Paul and my teenage brother were passing a fifth of Gentleman Jack back and forth, while Gisele and I shared a cylindrical flask of tequila. Ours was one of the few stretches of private beach anywhere in Roosevelt County, but walk only a hundred yards and the shore belonged to everyone. Distant cries of reveling children echoed across the wide public space of the flat sand stretch. George could probably identify the voices, friends of his, but there was important family business to discuss: the wedding.

It was only six days away, so there wasn't much left to plan. Jill had taken care of nearly everything. The entire ceremony, from the service to the reception, would be conducted at various locations around the National Park. Our home was to be overfull with guests. Everything was in place for an ideal wedding. What hadn't been planned: the bachelor party. Paul was no good with setting up anything in advance, and Jim Harrison was even worse. I was pretty good at throwing a party, but I wasn't in the best shape, and Paul didn't trust me with such events because I was crazy. So the responsibility fell to a sixteen-year-old, George.

"Two half-words for you," George said, pushing fingers through his brown mop. "Co-ed."

Paul fingered his guitar, tapping the frets to make notes without plucking. He looked up only when George passed him the whiskey. "Of course it will be co-ed," Paul said. "The Murray's girls will be there."

"Who are the Murrays?" Gisele asked, suspicion in her wide-set eyes.

"Murray's is a titty bar in the Heights," Paul said.

Gisele curled her fish lips into an Elvis sneer. The idea of us brothers fraternizing with a gaggle of strippers seemed too much for her to bear.

"They're traveling as far as Ann Arbor for the occasion?" I asked.

A bullwhip crack, skin on skin, as Gisele slapped my bare forearm. I winced in pain. Paul laughed nervously and George shook his head. I did the same, bangs strobing my vision like a zoetrope.

Paul recovered from his steady chuckling to say, "We're not even sure where it's going to be. Or when."

"There's really only one night left: dirty Thursday," George said. "And would you have it anywhere but here? No."

"On the beach, everything is permitted," I said.

"If you cheat on me I will kill you," Gisele whispered in my ear, breath hot as a lake of sulfur. "I mean it. I'm capable of murder."

"Cut that lover whisper shit," Paul said. "It's too cutesy." At this point I almost wanted to reach for the fifth of bourbon, but I let him swig it instead. Needing something to distance myself from the deepening disturbance of what was unfolding, I took a long pull of tequila and lit a cigarette. Paul asked for one and I handed it off.

"What I'm saying is, why settle for Murrays?" asked George. "Why not go get some Canadian strippers?"

"And do what?" Gisele asked. She was as lewd as any of us around that fire, but she often pretended to be purer than she was.

"You know for a smart girl you have a real impoverished imagination. Let's just say those girls let you touch," Paul said.

Gisele, to me, under her breath: "If I gave a shit about that trashy bitch he's marrying I might say something, but…"

"This stays on the beach," Paul said, pointing at Gisele with an incline of the whiskey in hand.

"I was just saying that," my woman said. "You can trust everyone here."

The figure rose over the green roll of a bladed dune, a black silhouette against the cyan of a sky whose westward expansion still held a fade of the day's light. I need only see the shape of the head, with its beret cocked over hair, to know that my tormentor had returned. For some reason he was carrying an acoustic guitar in a black gator-skin case. I thought I was hallucinating right there, that the medication I'd taken to taking again was of no use. But the corduroy on thighs squeak of his imported loafers on sugar sand was enough to turn Gisele's head in his direction.

"One keg-soaked odyssey for an out of town orgy," George said.

Their backs were to the gentleman of wealth and taste, and Paul was finger-picking his Guild, playing a Nick Drake tune note for note correct. Though I knew what he was playing to be written for a capoed guitar, Paul's fingers were so long and nimble that he was able to use his index as a capo and finger the entire thing with one less digit. He looked at me, expecting me to sing, but my eyes were stapled to the man behind him.

"Poor troubadour killed himself before he reached Bombay," were the first words I heard the German say. "Now Nick Drake's a tree in my bleeding forest."

Gisele looked at me strangely, as if I could protect her from my tormentor. She seemed to know that I recognized him. "I'm sorry to trouble you folks, but I couldn't help but overhear your tentative plans for this extravaganza, and I wanted to offer my services."

"Go away," I hissed through clenched teeth.

George looked at me, raising an eyebrow and stroking his three-day stubble.

"Who the fuck are you?" Paul asked.

I feared for the answer, knowing my worst suspicions would be confirmed.

"Woland is the name." Gisele had never read Bulgakov or Goethe, so the reference was lost even on her. But the introduction confirmed everything I feared, and, I began to shake so intensely that my teeth chattered sixteenth notes. "I just so happen to have a peace offering." He passed Paul a vial that glinted in firelight. Yellow powder. "Fresh from Afghanistan. My friends are doing great work there."

Paul packed the yellow powder in to the recessed filter of his cigarette and snorted it. He rocked back onto his elbows, and George saved the guitar from hitting the sand.

"You got any speed to go with this ball?" Paul moaned after a silent minute.

"Oh, I have friends in Columbia, too."

Paul roused himself and twinkled another Nick Drake song, at ease with the stranger already.

George was looking more and more confused by the second. He kept scanning the beach, clearly unable to experience the devil before us.

"I am the world's premier black magician."

Gisele snorted in apparent disbelief.

"I was hoping I could do some tricks at this little party you're planning."

"Shut your ass for a second and make with the coke," Paul said.

Woland laughed, deeply, his chortle as resonant and sustained as a didgeridoo. He produced a second vial and passed it off to my older brother. Paul packed the white powder in to the recessed filter of his cigarette and snorted it. He bobbed his eyebrows in approval.

"Get out of here," I said, almost squealing, so desperate I was to excise him from my life. "You are not welcome."

"Now you shut your ass, John. He's good people," Paul said.

"I have a horrible feeling about him," Gisele whispered into my ear.

"You're getting a migraine, that's all," Woland said. Now it was Gisele's turn to shudder. I had never stopped shaking, and the rhythm of her palsy matched mine.

She held her forehead with both hands, massaging her own temples as she asked, "How did you know that?"

"That's not all I know. Flowers will soon kill you."

"Don't threaten me you cheap piece of Eurotrash. The only thing that keeps you out a trailer park is your accent," she said, but her insult was softly spoken in a pained voice. Her headache seemed to be setting in.

"Leave," I plead of him. "Leave and never come back."

Woland only laughed. These were the words that Christ spoke during my reverie under the V Tree. His quotation was a mockery of everything that spiritual experience represented.

"To whom do you speak?" asked George of Paul, finally acknowledging the absence from one set of perceptions. "Am I missing something?"

"You're just lucky is all," I said. This seemed to annoy my younger brother even more, but instead of lashing out, he simply drank more whiskey, though only fifth a time. I would see younger and worse when I got to NYC AA.

"What kind of tricks do you do?" asked Paul, a shit-eating smile across his drugged-flat features as he lit his powdery cigarette.

"May I?" He reached for my cigarette. I shook my head. Paul handed his smoke to Woland. The middle-aged man took a long drag and held in the smoke. Then he blew a ring in the shape of a horned skull.

"That was weak," Paul said with a dismissive head shake.

Gisele nudged closer to me in the sand, and I inhaled her hair, thinking of my violated safe places: the beach, the woods, and the dry world.

Woland only laughed and kept laughing until his tossed the cigarette into the fire. The blaze turned into strangely green flame and then took the shape of our house, though its edges continued to flicker. Even the windows were rendered. The cigarette that had just been dropped stopped in midair, atop the house, and caught fire, its flames the proper color of fire. This conflagration held the shape of a childish symbol for a woman, as might be seen on the door to a restroom. Then it fell from the top of the fire house to the foundation. Synchronous with collision of the woman with the logs, Woland snapped and the blaze was only a blaze again.

"That's all kind of chintzy. Not a fan of fireworks. Explosions. Color. Big deal," Paul said. "But I guess if you're going to bring more drugs..."

"Look in your pack of cigarettes," Woland said at last.

"Full!" Paul said in wonderment. "Shit, guy, you're my new best friend."

"I have to go, John. My head. I'm seeing things," Gisele said as she stood and walked away as fast as she could without running. Her long legs made it easy for her to cross the beach with nimble speed. I knew she needed to be with me, but there was serious danger afoot, and I had to ascertain if the fire apparition had only been a vision of mine.

I met the gaze of my youngest brother, asking with my eyes if he had seen what I'd seen. George shook his head. "Who are you guys talking to?" Paul chided George and passed the Guild to the cardinal killer. As soon as he had it in his hands, he played a speed metal song, quickly and flawlessly. Paul was laughing as he said, "A great guy to have at a party."

I stood and pointed my finger at the furiously picking conjurer. "Stay away from my family." I walked away. My body had never felt so heavy. I heard footsteps following me, and started running. I was sure Woland was coming to get me. I felt a hand on my shoulder as my pursuer caught me from behind. I have never been much of a runner. Whipping around, fists clenched, I heard a familiar voice call for me to stop. It was only George, following me to talk in private.

"What the fuck?" George asked. "What am I missing?"

"Only what's killing us."

Probably assuming that he could not understand me because I was crazy as usual, George just shrugged. "I'm going to bed before I puke," George said. "Don't leave Paul alone there. You know how much he hates drinking by himself."

I nodded and turned back from the fire.

As I approached I heard incredible music. The devil had given Paul back his Guild and taken an ancient, mint Gibson out of the alligator case. They were playing. That word sounds insufficient for what was transpiring, however, played sounds as though this were the work of child prodigies. But Paul was no impatient gun in some band of the week. Rather he was holding his own with the Devil.

Woland sang a spiritual and seemed to ache with every word:

> Nobody knows the trouble I've seen
> Nobody know but Jesus
> Nobody knows the trouble I've seen
> Glory Hallelujah

They were trading leads over a standard twelve-bar progression. Blues had always bored me but this was redder than blues could hope to be. The man and the monster seemed to be in contest with each other, if only because each lead line seemed to trump the other. As had been the case with Jerry Garcia, what he took seemed to take him in an identifiable musical direction – you could tell what he was on just by his style.

Paul always did his best work on cocaine but the heroin seemed to have mellowed his frenetic style to the end that he sounded better than he ever had. There looked to be no end until, on one of Paul's turns, Woland played in unison with Paul's entirely improvised line. It was impossible and beautiful, and it broke my brother, so that after that cycle they finished at once, and even the waves seemed to gasp and then go silent as their impossible

Dry World

resonance hung, its fade sounding as though a cathedral had been
built around us and in its chamber we heard the reverb of God.

Chapter 19

Island Swamp

New York

Brian stunk when we met. He hadn't bathed since our frolic through the feculent waters of Central Park's Lake in the smallest hours of that morning. The odor was that of a rain-wet dog that had been rolling in roadkill. Sweating tourists were turning their reddening necks. Shopping models were flaring their impeccable nostrils. If I were capable of feeling, I would have been ashamed. But the drugs were so much with me that I just didn't care about anything other than that he had arrived with Billie.

Brian kept singing two lines I wrote over and over, seeming to mock me and enjoying it: I was born in paradise but I was raised in hell.

Finally he started talking at me rather than singing to me, this time about a sordid, sober misadventure. I wasn't listening. I already felt Billie's nearness, and my entire being was focused, but dimly, dimly. The intensity of my two-day whirl hadn't faded in my heart, but my undermined brain could no longer muster the blinding effulgence of only a few hours before. I was a slim fraction of the charmer who had wooed her, and no match for the man at her side in the state I was in.

She looked better than ever, and worst of all, they looked happy together. She was reading his palms, running over his furrows the fragile fingers that had stroked me the day before. I couldn't even summon jealousy. I just resigned myself to the inevitability of their relationship. That's how actively passive the medication made me. I was ready to walk right by them without a word when the end of Brian's nearly shouted sentence caught them.

"... and that's why I took a shit on his face."

Billie screwed his features into an Elvis smirk. She flicked a red tipped block of hair and said, "That is why I love you so much, Bri; because I know you said what I think you said. Who was the lucky boy?"

I might have been taken aback by their intimacy, but I was deeply drugged. As such, I had only a distant yearning for some sugar of my own, buried under the figurative tons of too many milligrams of downers. In my state, I couldn't even summon a questioning look to explain their sudden closeness.

Yet Billie read my muted body language nonetheless. "Are you okay, John?" She addressed me from a distance, and, at last, like a dinosaur in a cartoon, slow to respond, this distance hit me and hurt badly. We had only been close for a matter of hours, but we'd spoken of such lifelong expectations that I'd been caught into her future world and now that future all smelled like a bullshit session. I looked to Brian and he looked to me, and we hugged as we always did. I was hoping Billie would take the cue and at least wrap her arms around me, press her breast to my chest, perhaps, but I was graced with no such affections. She only stroked Brian's forearm as he launched into a rerun of the recollection I'd just heard.

"We call it the three nuggets story," Brian said. I buried my face in my hands and didn't remove them until the story was over. Brian continued: "See, there's this rule in my basement that if you fall asleep with your shoes on, we can fuck with you however we want. So my friend Tito goes to sleep that way and my brother Plato says, Brian, there's no way you'll take a shit on his face, and then he made it a bet, so I had to do it. Not for money, see, but for pride. Now Tito was way drunk and straight passed out, so even though the first nugget hit his eyelid he didn't budge. The next one hit his cheek and the last one landed on his lips and just stayed there. So we left it till he woke. And this best part is, I was sober, so I remember it all."

"Wait," Billie interjected, "wait, you did that in recovery?"

"Well, yeah, before I had John as a sponsor." He slapped my back and I thought of the progress he'd made under my care. As far as I knew, he hadn't done anything like that since we'd had our current relationship. The worst action he'd taken was to slap a mugger with a hot slice of pizza. There's a saying in AA – progress, not perfection. We are not saints, but we can and do get better.

I grabbed the metal tattooed into Brian's forearm and squeezed it as he said, "You might be the only reference he has for what sober people are like and that could kill the kid you shit on." I was being serious now, but they pair met me with incredulity, as if I didn't understand the sophomoric humor. Rather, I was vainly asserting my role as sponsor and coming off as a killjoy.

Now it was Billie's turn to bury her face in her hands. It stayed covered just long enough for her to miss Brian's fracture. In an instant he went from warm and childish to cold and killing. Perhaps it was the rough contact that broke him into the spell. Whatever it was, Brian was no longer Brian, or not the Brian I had loved until he loved himself. His spine stiffened until his towering frame was at its imposing apex, six inches above me. Slight shivers, like my medication shakes, courses through his fingers in pulses. His eyes slivered into cutting slices of ebony. I put a hand on his stomach and he knocked it away. The sleeper had awakened, and the sleeper was ready to kill.

When Billie pulled her head out of her hands, Brian was reaching for the ivory knife slung in the back of his studded belt. And I swear by all that I believe in that Woland passed just then, together as pedestrians trying their best to ignore the unfolding spectacle. Each had a Starbucks cup in hand, and the devil tipped his iced coffee at me as he winked his one blue-gold eye. He must have been looking for me. I didn't connect the Starbucks cup in Brian's hand with a rendezvous to arm the maniac.

Everything might have gone to shit then, but Brian recognized the Devil and stepped after him as a way of escape. Brian never even unsheathed his knife before We all ran downtown, me leading her by the hand. This left a shaking, murderous child swinging his white blade while running down Broadway on a tourist's afternoon, after us or away from Woland. I could not know. When we made the train, Brian eyed me strangely, like a man sleeping with his eyes just open a crack. "Do you remember that?"

"Of course," he said, "I was just telling the three nugget story." It was clear then that that was as far as his consciousness was willing to go, that another Brian, the Brian of meat cleavers in Central Park, had found a way through the inhibitions of a sober mind and could return at the flash of a provocation.

I looked to Billie, her hand in mine and for the first time since I'd told her I was having an episode, her nose twitched. "I know somewhere safe and quiet for thinking. Together, the three of us jogged to the Canal Street station and caught the Q to Park Slope. We made it to St. John's Place at express speed and I called mentor while heading up the steps to the street. The stop was so close to the place, though, that Roger's phone was still ringing when he opened the door and let us in.

"Billie, this is my boss, Roger Abbey," I said.

"Roger A!" I know you."

"The Ease and Comfort group," my mentor said. He was sober after all, and apparently the pair knew each other from meetings.

"I never put it together," she said.

"Those jacket photos of me are twenty years old," he explained.

Roger was the father figure of young people's AA, at least in the sense that he sponsored somewhere around ten young men even though he rarely went to youth AA meetings himself.

Dry World

"I can't believe you're my date to prom," she said and then all this.

I barely heard the second clause in that sentence, which seemed to make their relationship sound fairly safe. I only knew my boss was taking my lover to the recovery dance of the year and I was not. The world of young AA in New York really is that small and incestuous. I should have known the principal over us all would know a beauty like Billie.

This whole time Roger just stared at me with a smirking twist to his mouth, frozen like a wax statue honoring smugness. I knew then that he had brought me to these people to teach me some lesson he could never drive home through subtle, meaningless hallucinations. This beast was not a hallucination. He was the wraith that speaks to all of the living who were mad like me, and mad like the monster charging us just then.

"Billie going with you?" he asked. "I've got to stay with her," he said.

The bowling ball covered in tattoos and plastic spikes rolled into the townhouse, his body knocking aside thin white pins as if they were just that, and not people in the way of his score. Brian trashed the foyer, only the foyer, and then fled. The whole time, though, Roger just laughed and then told me that I should get used to strikes such as this if I planned on being of service.

Just then I got it. I knew the answer to the hardest assignment. "Roger, I write to be of service to God and my fellow man. That's it. That's fucking it."

"Correct," Roger said, the right corner of his smirk rising to make half a smile. "Now start writing like that."

Chapter 20

For the Rest of your Days

Michigan

I awoke the morning after Woland befriended Paul to a strange message from her. She had called me around dawn, just before she left Roosevelt to head back across the state. I knew she was going early, she had to open her boutique, but I didn't think she would leave the kind of words I was hearing. "I can't come to the wedding or I will die. I saw it last night in the Migraine. I'll call you someday, when I'm ready."

Drastic action needed to be taken or I would lose her forever. This I knew in the heart that was pumping through my temples as I replayed the message to make sure it was real, make sure it was really her. I didn't yet believe in the truth of her migraine visions, or that the evil man who kept showing up in my woods could really foresee her flowery death. The whole situation seemed mad and maddening, and I needed to be the sane one for once and set her straight. There was a solution, I thought. If we just got engaged, everything would be okay. I was that foolish in the face of fate. All I thought I needed: my brother's car and my mother's ring.

Procuring these was simpler than it might sound. It was late in the morning on a Sunday, and my parents had gone to church. In their empty bedroom, I found the massive stone set in filigree on my mother's dresser, there instead of on her hand, as if she knew I might need it soon. They had dragged poor George with them to the service, but his blue Volvo station wagon was there. In his empty bedroom, I found the tied fly hung from a key ring on my brother's dresser, there and ready to be lifted.

The miles between Roosevelt and Ann Arbor passed as if someone else were behind the wheel and we were going there together. In my deluded state where I thought I was the sane one who would set my crazy world right, I fancied that it might be God himself really steering things. His will at work in my life, and the Volvo just a vessel of his ultimate mission: to see Gisele and me wed someday. I kept the ring on the passenger seat, in the middle, as if it were a person traveling along side me. I even buckled it in and spoke to it when someone else was driving poorly. It didn't speak back. I had been taking too many drugs for that kind of thing to work, but once, and only once, it interjected into one of my rants, one word: "One." And when I turned to look it was silent again.

At the point of the portal to the perpendicular universe, the trees parted as they always did, and the miniature skyscrapers of the dense little city still appeared majestic, not yet having been dwarfed by what I'd seen of the East. That future felt so near, the future of my life in New York, that as I passed into the shaded, tree-lined streets, windows down, folk strums blaring, I saw the ending to my book as clearly as I'd just seen the whole of my college town. So, instead of finding Gisele, I drove straight to a northward computer lab and, fixed in my chair for the next seven hours, wrote the last forty pages of my novel in one sitting, the keystrokes flowing like the turgid trickle of the nearby Huron River.

So it was dark when I left the closing lab, two hundred thirty-one pages of the most acidic, cutting piece ever to fray the knitting of my social circle. It all might have been academic if I'd left it as just that, printing, but before I left the lab, I ensnared myself in social network, blogging the whole manuscript. Then I sent out a hundred and forty-four recipient message for the world to see it as soon as possible. This, and her blistering reading speed, allowed Gisele to have finished what she hadn't read of that book when I showed up at O' Neill, a manuscript in one hand and an engagement ring in another.

I found her nestled into the corner of her bed, her computer open on her lap. Her door had been unlocked and I had strolled in as if the room were still mine alone. All while singing:

> And I want to miss you
> And I want to kiss you
> And I want to wish you the best
> For the rest of your days

She met my eyes with a teary wariness that I took for the positive impact of my self-published work. I kicked off my loafers and knelt onto the bed, genuflecting only one knee to strike the proposal pose. But first I dropped the manuscript onto the mattress, and it rippled the springs with its scattering bulkiness. Pages like flakes of ice queen tears blown in the fan's buzzing breeze. There, as my supposed masterwork went to pieces around me, I opened my clenched left fist and said only, "Will you..." before she snatched up the adornment and answered.

"Yes," kiss "yes," kiss," yes." Then, as she folded up the laptop with a click, she slid on the massive jewel with greedy speed. And it had been on only a second when she changed, a pallor falling over her countenance, as if she were short of breath, the blues in her nearly visual in their intensity. Her eyes had fixed on the mess of what had been the stacked pages of my book only moments before.

"I have something for you," I said, motioning to the blowing laser paper.

"I have something for you," she said, fingering the ring. I cocked an eyebrow and she cocked her fist. With her bejeweled hand, she struck my face, as hard as I had ever been struck by father or brother, and I felt the cut from the diamond like an insect stinging a tongue in a working honeycomb. There had been such heavenly sweetness before the sharp strike. As I held my reeling features, both hands over my face, I only heard her tirade.

"You wrote me into the book without so much as a warning. And I seem crazy, like you're saving me or something, not the other way around. Now everyone knows about my secrets. I mean, Chloe, she deserved it, she's a bitch, but me? I don't need this shit, John. I want you to take it off the Internet. Now. Right now. Or I'll throw this ring into the Huron. Then you can wipe that blood on your dick and fuck me."

So I acquiesced. I gave her my password to the website and she took it down for me, and then changed my password to make doing it again more difficult. She wrote a second email to the entire group and sent it with my name attached. Apologizing for publishing the book before it was ready. Of course, Chloe had read it in that lapse, saved a copy that would seal her hatred for me in a waxy shell no sun or time could melt. And she was the only other reader besides Gisele who mattered, if only because the book was perhaps crueler to Chloe than it was to Gisele.

My fiancé ripped the sheets off the old bed, scattering what hadn't blown around of my novel all around the room. That way, the diamond cut on my cheek wouldn't stain her new bedding as it had stained her previous set of sheets. Instead, she stained the mattress, her fingers grazing my wound to mark the fake satin with strange shapes of browning red while we coursed the pleasure and pain of hateful sex as my phone kept vibrating. My brother was missing a car; my mother was missing a ring; Chloe was missing a heart, but nothing mattered as long as there was juice enough in me for the blood, semen, sweat and tears to be one.

When the warring storm passed like so much fallen rain, and we were in the gutters flowing downhill, she curled into the small of my arm and we discussed what music would be played at our wedding reception. I waited for her to slip into a troubled, twitchy sleep before I pulled clothing over my bloodstained body and walked through the house red-skinned as a soldier fresh from a melee. I drove home to Roosevelt without so much as a rest stop to wash my face. Dawn broke behind me as I chased the last blackness of the setting stars.

My parents were waiting on the wide front porch as I pulled up in the station wagon and stepped out of the car. My mother screamed as if I were the walking corpse of her son. I must have looked something like that. My father hung his fat head as it shook, unable to meet my bleary eyes. Paul and George came running to the curdling sound of my mother's shriek, roused from their indoor vigil for my disappearance. I looked intractable; I felt invincible. "Who did this to you?" my mother asked, through a gasp.

"Gisele," I said. "We're engaged." And only then, at the good news, did my mother begin to cry.

Chapter 21

Another Spring Has Come

New York

A large, square pane of glass rested on the wood blocking off a construction site. I only heard it shatter behind me. Brian had kicked it in with steel toes and was standing with a leg on either side of the pane's frame. When he let out a squeaky laugh, he resembled a toddler enlarged by some sci-fi machine: plump, reckless, and immature in every sense. We ran afterward, Sylvia and I did at least, but Brian plodded at the same pace as before. As we reached a stair down to the six train, we heard another crash. Brian had knocked over a garbage can and was jumping around with his arms aloft, having won the prizefight against boredom. He bellowed a tenor note, a blare that faded as Sylvia rushed down the stairs, our hands sliding down the slick metallic railings on either side. We were on our way to the most bizarre party in town.

My ears were then filled with the rumble and peal of a train coming to rest. My tie fluttered as I sped up. Sylvia and I ran and this time, I looked back to see that Brian ran with us. His strides were long and stretching as fast as he could make them go. He beat me to the gate. Only I fumbled with the turnstile, and Brian and to hold the door of the car so that I could slip through. A blast of hot and then cold air hit me, the side effect and effect of the train's air conditioning. The chill of this raised gooseflesh on me. We sat in silence. He rested his wide head on my shoulder, throwing a few dreadlocks onto my face in the process. I spit out the chunks of hair and smiled at Sylvia, opposite us and reading a

Roger Abbey novel. Her leg was twitching and ticking out a muted rhythm on the floor. The night's energy was already moving through us.

It was a time when people wore suits on Saturdays. I was in seersucker. It was far too hot even for that, but my blazer covered most of the sweat collecting around my arms and behind my back. The tight curves over Sylvia's wide bones made her look like a pinup in the years when curves were more important than abs. She kept whipping the long dive of her fluttering hair when a vent would blast it with cold air. Brian wore jeans and a jean vest that showed the exposed robotics of his arms. We felt ice cold: there was a sense that we were the coolest motherfuckers on the planet as we slid close together and Sylvia patted the heads of her boys. I closed my eyes and got lost in thoughts broken only by the disembodied voice of the train when it announced its stops. I heard the shout of DJs to come.

As the speaker squawked its slightly fuzzy words, I had a thought that came to me often in my New York years: I became overwhelmed with by the presence of what we as people had built; everything from the tiles to the tracks had been put in place by a hand, sometimes using machines, other times using fingers, but always constructing a world. I sometimes felt this whole place was a bible: crafted by countless authors over hundreds of years and holy, at least to me. The books were all around us. There was a verse even for the cheesy ads above and the cold, smooth seats that slipped under me.

I heard the snorts and cackles before I saw the face. There was only one laugh like that that I had ever known. I jerked in shock, knocking Brian's head upright. Terror flayed me and I held what guts I had in place, hoping their courage would get me through. I looked to my left to confirm what I felt would be inevitable. I wasn't ready but the time for our encounter had come. I felt nauseous and jerked my face away, thudding my cheek against the plastic window and wrapping the exposed side with my hand so that no one could see me. As the seconds passed, my palm began to sweat and damped my face.

Chloe was on the train.

I'd last seen her a few days after the Republican Convention, in early September of 2004. I'd run into her at a protest. Neither of us were participants; we were just passing through the marching throng to get to respective appointments. As people flowed around us, I begged for a coffee date, all but yelling to be heard. I never wanted to see her again but I had to make my ninth step amends to her. That was best done in person. I had to tell her it was for AA for her to agree. She told me her number was the same and we met at a Starbucks. I mumbled my desire to set things right and she told me that the best way for me to do so was to never see her again. She then apologized for nothing specific and left me at my table near the door. The punishing heat of the day flowed toward me as she went through the entrance and disappeared into an uptown crowd.

I was under strict orders from my old sponsor to follow Chloe's wishes and stay away from her, but she had appeared and was sitting only a few feet from me on the opposite bench. I heard her dorky laughter again and even thought I could smell her lavender scent through Sylvia's noxious patchouli. She was reading the same Roger Abbey novel as Sylvia and was enjoying it aloud. My face still hidden, I cracked my fingers slightly, just wide enough to see that she was pregnant and beaming at a beautiful man beside her. She then looked right the monstrous man to my right.

Brian had just blown his nose into his palm and was showing me the best booger he had harvested. "Blowing smoke through my nose makes them better," he said, and then gave me a quick nod.

I looked straight ahead but could see Chloe turn her disgusted gaze away from him. I just looked at the side of her face in the hospital-like lighting of the car. She then looked right at me looking at her, but her focus quickly shifted to a point very distant but in the same line of sight that I was. She tossed her hair, its color and shine like fired clay. I didn't see her switch the cross of legs. I didn't see whether she had started shaving those legs. I didn't see the way her thighs stayed tight in her jeans even with the baby above. I told myself I saw nothing until I looked back as we left the train at the Astor Place stop. As the train pulled away, a baby began to screech and wail.

I could only watch my feet until we were at the street. One sneaker after the other, crossing a floor tinted by scum. When I looked up and around at the west edge of the East Village, I found Sylvia staring at me, her eyes deeply sad, as if my feeling were contagious. In a way it must have been. "What's wrong, John?" Sylvia asked.

"I'm tired," is all I said. In reality, Chloe had brought to mind a heart rending tune:

Dry World

We met in spring some years back
When I still had thick skin
Another spring has come round
And washed away my sin
You're distant as an actress
In a film I'm not in
But what's undone must stay undone now anyhow
What's undone must stay undone now.

"Wake up then!"

The night was breathing hard and wet and damp. Chatter
rattled around as if we were in the audience of a theater whose
lights had yet to dim. That Saturday night was a week exactly
before the sober prom. Saint Mark's Place was clogged with
honking traffic and its sidewalk constricted by tourists who kept
looking up. There were no towers or stars in the East Village sky
but they looked up regardless. Brian led the way and was
shouldering into the occasional punk among the dads with fanny
packs. He was looking to smash more than glass apparently. Luckily
the other guys covered with metal and tattoos shied away from
messing with our monster. The throngs thinned as we passed east
and crossed between two trees on the uptown side, jaywalking
diagonally onto the park side of the Avenue A. Tompkins Square
Park opened ahead, bright green leaves hanging a few feet above
the wrought iron fence. Brian ran his fingers over the top of that
waist-high, black fence. As the park passed, I spotted the line of
people waiting to get into our destination, and someone yelped like
a rodeo rider. The sticky wetness under my suit was near
unbearable and Sylvia was glowing on the verge of sweat beads.
We would all be more comfortable when we got inside, and at last
we were inside the beating walls of the bar's heart.

Brian had managed to get in with a fake ID he had never used for drinking, only for nights like this. It was going to be some night. We were already feeling the bass in the line to check out belongings. Sylvia spoke to me at a normal volume and it was drowned out, so she shouted, but that was drowned out, too. I shrugged and she shrugged and we let whatever she had to say go unsaid.

It was time to check for Brian and I to check our pants anyway. This was the underwear party, after all. In the glint of a black light the skin of my bare legs almost glowed. Sylvia got out of checking her pants because she wasn't wearing any – she was in a dress for a reason. I checked my blazer as well and we were unsheathed and ready to cut. The night became flashes then – the strobe light slideshow of a party exploding over and over. On the walls were clips of Bollywood movies inter cut with hard core pornography. No one bothered to watch. There was enough skin in the place already.

Yet there was more skin to come. At three AM on the mark, a six foot Arab transvestite who called herself Scheherazade began a twisted contest. This was usually a competition to determine the best looking person in the place. Men and women alike, naked and getting there, climbed a slim stage where Scheherazade was claiming she's sucked a thousand and one cocks and was ready for more. I looked for Brian to see his contagious laugh rumble through him and saw him nowhere until I saw him on the stage. Between his tattoos and a penis whose immensity I never wanted to know, Brian became one of two finalists in the contest for the hottest body. The other finalist had him beat on charm, however. A naked Filipina with a Buddha belly was singing an eighties song about an

Dry World

Asian girl into Scheherazade's microphone while playing with her tits. Across her belly was written, "Star Six Nine."

"I have to know your name," Scheherazade said just before setting off the crowd for the final judging.

"Star Six Nine!" she screamed. The crowd roared.

"And where are you from?"

"Star Six Nine!" The crowd roared even louder.

Next Scheherazade took Brian's oversized life into her hands for three shakes and squealed with honest, falsetto joy. "I didn't think it could get any bigger!"

The crowd roared in a high pitched way, it becoming clear that the women were more into Brian than the men.

"So who's it going to be, assholes? Star Six Nine..."

A cheer that shook God rose.

"Or the telephone cord?"

More laughter than applause followed this.

"I need to really hear you, bitches!"

In the cheering contest that followed, Star Six Nine easily won. Scheherazade presented her with a trophy made of a giant dildo on a cheap, unfinished hunk of pine.

"It's not as big as telephone cord's... but it'll have to do."

The contest was over and the night was winding down. I had forgotten about my love woes past and future until a song came on that had played on the first mix tape that Chloe had made for me. Everyone seemed to love it. I decided to split for the open-air stairwell and smoke under the steps down to the subterranean club. A bit of the night chilled me as I walked out in checkered boxers. A front had gone through and air was cooling for the first time in what seemed like weeks. The thud of the nightspot traveled even through the concrete front and I tried to determine the song by the bass and drums that were the only parts passing through. It was a disco beat, that much could be felt. Suddenly there was the scent of lavender in the air. It strengthened in intensity, pushing through everything into memories of Chloe. Then I turned around to place it and saw Billie and Roger. It was not my night.

Roger's knees were bumpy and his legs somehow whiter than mine. He wore tight white boxer briefs that, uncomfortably enough, showed the average size of his junk. There was a lot of that at the underwear house party; you were always best served to look up unless you were sure that looking down would be worth it. For me it was, for there I saw the separated inner curves of Billie's upper thighs. Her underwear was plain white satin. I looked up and saw her gazing at me blankly. I tried to read that blankness, feel around for some kind of feeling shining from her. I finally felt as though she were pretending I was not there. I shivered, and my knees knocked together and kept knocking. My head got very hot and I thought of Chloe looking through me as well.

Dry World

I only waved Billie and Roger from afar and turned away. It was too loud for us to talk from that distance, and there were perhaps a dozen people in three cliques separating us. There was nothing unusual about Roger being here, especially his being outside smoking his small cherry cigars. Most nights that he came here, and he came here most every weekend, he would barely ever go inside. He didn't need a drink. All he needed was a place to stand and smoke where he could meet men with silly stories and women with needy hearts. I heard Roger's laugh then, a lowly honking noise, like a large trombone. It was drowned out when the door to the club swung open and Brian stepped out.

He looked as surprised as I was to see Billie here. She only liked dancing naked in her apartment. Her words. Perhaps the bare legs were close enough for her now. Regardless, Brian all but exploded on her. I could hear him. He was screaming every synonym for a vagina that I had ever heard and a few I had only read in books. The savageness in him was all the more terrifying because I had heard his entire personal history and knew about the two men he'd hurt, perhaps murdered, back in his Brooklyn crackhead days. As the situation worsened and a bouncer appeared, I began to approach the three of them, until someone pulled back my arm. I whipped my head and saw Woland with bare legs and a toothy grin. "It's too bad she won't live forever," he said as I pulled at his arm, trying to get away. Then he disappeared and I fell to the sticky concrete floor, pushed over by the force with which I'd been trying to escape my Devil. It was then that I first saw Billie killed in my mind. Her face appearing in her stoop above the geraniums in the window box, and then the tattooed arms around that face and squishing it into mush as if it were soft as a grape. I really saw this when I closed my eyes, in the way that I sometimes see my worst fears in little hallucinations. I opened my eyes and several minutes had passed, my trance disposing of them. I was only roused when I felt someone take my hand. It was Sylvia. Billie had texted her and we were leaving.

The cliques had spread into a semicircle under the stairs to the street. Their whispers could be seen but not heard. The bass and drums made it that way. I broke through the circle where three bouncers were wrestling with my massive punk friend and not getting very far, between Brian's size and rage. No one wanted to call the police because there were naked people and hard drugs all over the inside. So they just gathered their forces and pulled the runner up in the hot body contest up the stairs, his boots thudding on a few of the steps as he was taken up. The book was almost over; only a few more verses had yet to be written.

Brian was flat on this back next to the curb, and beside him was Star Six Nine. She'd been leaving tonight, dildo trophy under her arm, when she saw a potential friend on the ground and decided to connect with him. Somehow he was laughing with her as they had on stage, Brian's mood swung like a reaper's scythe, grimly culling someone soon to be a corpse. So there Star Six Nine sat next to Brian, the top of the painted numbers still exposed above her bible-black dress.

Chapter 22

Pleased to Be Plucked

Michigan

Chrome shone in the sun. Bright colored cars were scattered around the party bus. Many had doors flung wide, revealing stern young women issuing the last warnings they could to their partners. Peach index fingers were shaken. Thick and almost thick heads of men shook and shook and then nodded and nodded. I wished then that Gisele had been there to drop me off in her beige Saab. Her warnings would be cruel and severe and I wanted be hurt by her again. At that thought, I took a long pull of vodka from my great grandfather's flask. The cars began to recede into the afternoon, catching pulses of reflected sun that made them twinkle like movie star eyes.

The last was then gone, and the men rumbled into the party bus. The vessel filled up potential disasters who moved wildly. We were that frenetic and white and messy. Hairy, sunburned arms were flung upward with hands locked into devil horns and then shaken. One fellow just kept jumping in place in the aisle. We had barely begun to drain the two half barrels of Michigan micro-brews, but the anticipation of how wild were going to be already had several guys playing the role of the drunks they would soon be.

On a boombox, someone put on a song I wrote called "Get Fucked Up" and fists were being pumped. Voices filled the sticky air with exhaust and the din of interweaving lectures. Chatter can be

difficult for me to deal with. I get paranoid. I take words that I hear
or I think I hear from the conversations around me and piece
together sentences about myself. I become convinced that
everyone is talking about me. The only way I could think to get rid
of that feeling was to drink more. My flask was empty, so I reached
into my satchel pulled out one of the two fifths of vodka that would
get me through the day, and hopefully the next morning.

On the bus: Stevie, Paul's doubles partner at Roosevelt
Shores High School, who had been disqualified from the state finals
because of a DUI the night before; Rick, with whom Paul used to
come up with elaborate routines for dances at Roosevelt Shores
Middle School and was now a grad student in Philosophy at Dover
State; Henry, a mushroom dealer, a black hippie who used to take
Paul to concerts in his white VW camper van and was the best
guitar player of the bunch, and there were many guitar players in
the bunch; Ted, who had a seven year old daughter from a one
night stand during his freshman year at University of Michigan and
had never missed a child support payment thanks to his job at the
Roosevelt Post Office; Don, our cousin who shot Paul with an air
rifle during a family reunion on the Little Agawatta River, and was
now a theology student at Princeton; four other members of the
tennis team, three other drug dealers, two cousins by marriage, Jim,
George, me, and a dude in an Afro wig whom nobody seemed to
know.

Khaki cargo shorts and golf shirts were a sort of uniform.
Everyone wore them except George and me. I stuck out as usual.
My hair was a purposeful mess and my sparse whiskers patched
my chin with a dithered gray. I wore girl's jeans that were cuffed
and a western shirt with small red, tan and navy checkers. My feet

breathed through low top All Stars whose white rubber was smeared with dirt. I looked, in short, as a hipster was supposed to look in the summer of 2003.The only other exception to the khaki rule was George, who wore a white Tyvek jumpsuit and a Chinese fighter pilot helmet, both of which he'd ordered off the internet. I guess he was trying to start spaceman chic. Everyone seemed ready to fly except for me. I just wanted vodka and Gisele.

Jim Harrison had organized the surprise journey with exceptional forethought. In addition to securing the kegs and the bus and the driver, he had added a moment of flair that was all him. The first step of Jim's plan was to abduct the groom. He called my brother's foreman at their construction site and told him that a dozen men with nylons on their heads would be grabbing Paul and jamming him into a burlap sack. The operation went smoothly. I had worried because Paul had been working to build a new Wal-Mart, and I wasn't sure what sort of corporate bullshit might stop us. But with a boom box on Jim's shoulder blaring the a spy show theme song, he directed his bland troops with precision and Paul was sacked quickly. My older brother must have assumed it was a stunt, because he didn't throw any uppercuts and barely struggled inside the burlap. As the thick fabric was pulled away from his head, laughter that had been muffled became clear and loud. It was on.

Our destination was Windsor, Ontario. Just across the Ambassador Bridge from downtown Detroit is a town sleazier in many ways than the urban blight on the American side. Because of its legal gambling and prostitution, Windsor is the sin town for Michigan. It even has three significant advantages over Vegas: its drinking age is 19, strippers can be nude in bars, and, most importantly, these strippers can be touched. Paul would be able to fondle and George would be able to drink. Though no one was stopping my younger brother from getting drunk on this side of border, his participation in the bar night was important to us all. The three of us brothers were together then, with Paul between George and me and arms around all shoulders. It might have been a moment for a photograph, except that Jim had barred all cameras from the excursion. There were too many girlfriends to consider.

Neither were there supposed to be any drugs, but from the smell of things this stipulation wasn't being upheld. The smoke, from cigarettes and God knows what else, showed shafts of the sun as it lowered behind us. Rebellious yells cheering on blunt smoking would rise every few seconds, mostly from the tennis team. The guy in the Afro wig never seemed to be without an oversized, under-inflated balloon in his hands, having brought along nitrous oxide for refilling whipping cream or getting a fifteen second buzz. Even Jim had a spoon in a bag of white and was taking bumps. The night was beginning in the late afternoon. Only I wanted to spend it naked in my old room with a bottle and Gisele.

We made it no further than Fowlerville before a serious problem shut down the progress. The bathroom was full of piss and the guys still had almost a hundred miles to go. We pulled onto the country roadside opposite a gas station and the driver, after several bribes, found some kind of hose and started dumping urine into the gravel. The sun was setting behind the bus, one of those sunsets where it stays yellow almost to the end, and a steady wind shuffled a field and its trees seen from the roadside. I found my first fifth empty already. George had taken two pulls from it, but otherwise I had drunk the lot of it. I held the bottle up to that yellow light and spears of rarefactions shone spotted light. I dropped the bottle on the empty seat away from the window and was glad I wasn't on this pissing side of the bus.

Apparently I wasn't the only one who'd gone through a lot of booze. Afro wig started a chant that caught on, first with my family, then with the rest, of "Beer! Beer! Beer!" The second half-barrel was all but empty. Jim and my cousin Don were conferring with the seriousness of a nuclear disarmament summit. The world needed to be saved from certain disaster. So we pulled into the small service station that stood opposite the piss puddle. There were only four cases of cold beer in the place. After a multicolored flash of credit card after credit card, we bought them out of beer, leaving only two lonely six-packs of near-beer to taunt the next buyer who might come in. The herd had their lemming juice and were ready to head off the cliff.

Detroit rose all at once. I was very drunk by then, nodding out, and after such a nod, a snapped up my head and we were in a city. It was almost night then, and the skyscrapers were largely dark. Consequentially, there were more stars than I thought there would be. I thought then of Gisele's rhapsodies about her hometown, songs of praise of wonder at the dramatic history of this city, and how it foreshadowed the fate of America. This last bit made no sense until years later, when we all collapsed. Cars flew around us, their drivers perhaps frantic to escape the blight. The interstates were flowing into each other like tributaries into the Detroit River. At last the suspending towers of the bridge rose, red flashing atop them. The cables looked like hanging strings of Christmas lights, and I watched them blur above as we went on our way.

At the border, the man in the Afro wig began to scream about bombs. A few of the other dudes got into this as well. Paul's doubles partner, who by then had his golf shirt tied up as a girl at car wash might tie hers to reveal midriff, just kept yelling, "Terror!" over and over. Paul himself found the boom box and started up the spy show theme again. The insanity of the crowd struck me even in my stupor. Here we were, a giant target packed with drugs, and these fools acted as though security was going to hit its bulls-eye. I'm the kind of guy with a sense of humor sick enough to laugh at a nine-eleven joke, but this was just stupid. It might have flown in the nineties, but the world had become more uptight by then.

Jim seemed to understand this and swatted the Afro wig off the loser getting us into trouble. "Who the fuck are you anyway?"

"I sold that guy over there the kegs and he said I could come," said Afro wig.

Jim threw a half-full can of beer at this clerk and a tempered cheer rose from the Tennis players.

George took off his fighter helmet and walked up to me. "Hope your bowels are loose, sir, because they are about to get explored." He didn't wink after this joke. Instead, he whistled with his teeth and most of the men quieted down. The hush was just enough for us to hear the order to be searched. Out came the plastic bags. The dealers, two tennis players, the doubles partner, and Afro wig ate each at a bag. I had none and just swayed in my vodka daze. If I had to be bailed out, it would be a good reason to call Gisele in spite of her transgression. I was that mad for her.

Dry World

In came the dogs. For some reason they were using beagles. They smelled wet. Our bodies sat straight and calm in our chairs, but I turned my head and saw the welcome visage of the devil by the mumbling men. It was clear they couldn't feel him as he waved his hands through their heads. By the we were so silent that I could hear the dogs sniffing two rows ahead and behind. I was glad then that I only liked drinking. It kept me out of certain kinds of trouble. I felt like Lott not looking back. Somehow the beagles found nothing, but that wasn't the whole of our problem. The border cops seemed disturbed by our flippant references to terrorism. Detroit has America's largest population of Middle-Eastern immigrants, and that made the gravity of the situation denser and the tension tauter. Apparently it is some kind of crime to threaten to bomb something.

The officials were still conferring when a man in all gray approached behind them. Looking right into me, we waved his left hand through the heads of each officer as might a movie ghost. Apparently Woland had decided to enable our depravity. With the devil on our side, the man detaining us approached with a slack jaw that kept shuddering into chuckles as if he had been blasted with nitrous oxide at some dentist's office. When he took a place beside the driver at the head of the bus, he said, "I just wanted to tell you guys that if you pull this on the way back in you will be in a whole hell of trouble." He then paused. His neck was very thin and his head was very large, so it looked as though his head might tip over and hit his chest. "Welcome to Canada."

A roaring cheer rose from the men. A few jumped to their feet, arms in the air. We knew the ecstatic relief of survivors who have just found rescue from lifeboat. Even through the dulling cloud of vodka around my head I felt the emotion of the moment, until I saw him again. He stood looking straight into me, the ghost in my life's machine. Again he moved through a man, this time seemingly stepping inside an officer and disappearing altogether. I couldn't know if he had freed us. It was possible that the Canadians were laid back enough to let us skate through. I thought then about Woland's voice, the way it could shudder through my head, and it occurred to me again that he may have influenced those authorities whether or not they saw him.

We quickly found ourselves on a garish street beneath the pink and teal marquee for Leopard's. It looked as though it had been a movie theater in tamer times. A tall sign glowed in the twilight, shining the same pink and teal colors on the marquee. "You think there's a reason it's called that?" I asked.

Jim cocked an eyebrow and stroked his beard dramatically. "Probably because these pussies have spots on them," he said. "Let's go."

Just then my phone rang. Gisele was calling for the first time since our fight. I held up a finger to tell the guys I would be a minute. After a few awkward pleasantries, she found out that I was within an hour of her. "Get me out of here. Please," I said. I didn't want to be part of the international incident that surely would follow on the return, but I also burned to see her.

"I don't date guys who go to strip clubs," she said.

"I've never been in one," I said, "and I'll pace the sidewalk outside to keep it that way."

Dry World

So I walked up and down that block of Chatham Street, spending most of my time in front of a wide, red brick building with bright blue trim. The fake gaslight lamp posts were glowing in cones and once, I became bored enough to make shadow puppets. I was flapping a hawk when the beige Saab pulled up, humming like the old car it was.

Gisele looked the best I had ever seen her, though I wasn't sure if she looked any different, or if it were just my desire that cleaned her up so well. Her lips were the same thickness, and her eyes were the same color, and makeup was absent, but some aspect of her, perhaps her apologetic mildness, made her my fiancé again, even in spite of the violence.

George came up to me, taking a break from the place in time to see me leave. His jumpsuit had been unzipped seductively, and the plume of chest hair rising from it made him even stranger looking somehow. He looked at me warily, knowing what had happened with the ring. Then he stood behind her and put his hands on my shoulders, and began to coach me as if I were in the corner of a boxing ring. "Watch for the jab, and your best shot is to go for a left," he whispered close to my ear. I turned and he winked one eye, and then the other, and I got in the car.

On the drive home, I asked Gisele a few times to come to the wedding. Each time she would nod, but otherwise she insisted on silence for most of the night. When the silence felt strange, she would find a way to play music and fill the time. This pattern began in the car and continued when we got to the room. We listened to music and barely spoke. In a way, it was what our relationship had been all along – aesthetic and sexual chemistry with little other connect to speak of, literally. Gisele and I fucked and then she fell asleep while I spun on the floor. I didn't sleep well. I would close my eyes and drift into hypnagogia, where hallucinations are the rule for us all. There I would see her in a succession of disembodied components: just her neck, then just her right hand, then many more, all floating alone in blackness. The last one I saw was her nipple. This shot me up for the day.

At Five AM, I was awake and sitting up beside Gisele's bed, sipping vodka out of the bottle. There I watched the blue and black of the trees beside my old house. The boughs of the white pines moved the shadows slightly. There was a smell in the room, the smell of sex and women. I began to sing one of mine, softly to myself, "So swapped our parting words for smiles..." I would never sleep there again. The boards of the old house squeaked in warped spots as I left. For no reason I found myself reading everything on the bulletin board beside the door, multicolored signs about policy for the co-op and articles about music cut out of the New York Times. Then there were the photographs from film. These were too much. They began to move in silence. I had to go outside to break the spell, but before I did, I stared at the memory windows as they told stories that were already fading as might the music of a party left behind.

I was on the wide, round porch when the bus showed up just after dawn. I'm told the gang had been searched again on the way back in. Having already eaten all their baggies of drugs, there was nothing to find except for piles of cans and bottles covering the bus floor. Jim somehow talked them out of trouble by citing the "boys will be boys" precedent. The luck of a lenient border officer took them back into the country after making the men remove all the empties.

On the bus and riding, I was bright eyed in that way that brief spats of energy come early in the morning after a long night of drinking. As I watched my house, and then Ann Arbor, recede through the rear window, I couldn't help but sink in spirit. I wouldn't see that town again. College had ended with the bang and whimper of break-up sex. I was too old for recess and had to leave the playground behind. Only George and I were awake at that point. Sensing something off in me, he took off his fighter helmet and put it on me. I passed him the bottle, and then we swapped helmet for leftover bottle of Old Grand Dad, and then again, for an hour or so, until there was nothing left of the booze except for a desire for more. I found my fifth and sucked it dry as the rush hour traffic of Lansing moved around me with desperate purpose. There I sang of Saginaw, smoking a cigarette and wishing Michigan was a dream.

Chapter 23

Watch for Falling Rockers

New York

There was a blaze of taxis, flashing yellow and the passing away like the flicker of a plastic lighter to the right of Brian and me. We were in Chelsea, a predominantly gay neighborhood on the west side of Manhattan. This was not his first time in drag, and he seemed at ease in every way as my date to the sober prom. Brian walked beside me up Eighth Avenue in silence and a pale blue dress. The skirt was so long that he had to shuffle slightly. It was tight enough that the occasional puff of breeze could move none of it. He had a baby chin, and this coupled with his long dreadlocks made him look more feminine than I thought he would have. It helped that his makeup was elegant and precise. He even had a handbag, Chinese Prada, that appeared to contain only white crepe paper. Brian laughed maniacally for a long time, too long for comfort. When he composed himself, he pressed tight his lips and narrowed his eyes. The walrus ivory knife was in his cheap bag. He was flashing it, and it looked yellow compared to the crepe paper. Then it was gone, buried under the rippling crunch of the filling in his bag.

"You know what you do when you really resent someone, Brian?"

"Work the tenth step?"

"Just remember that someday that person will die."

Dry World

The sky above New York was touched with the barest white brushstrokes of cirrus clouds foretelling a coming rain. It was that time of year when the sun sets straight down Twenty-Fifth Street, casting the apartment complexes to its south in warm highlights. A random scatter of yellow squares showed lit places in those buildings. The brown brick stacks turn red except in shadows. Between eighth and ninth avenue there are trees on the sidewalk, young trees just old enough to shade patches of cement and asphalt the size of a child's merry-go-round. The last of the sun fell behind the edge of New Jersey, and all at once the streetlamps burst into hydroponic life, keeping the city alive even without the sun. Twenty-Third Street's bustle seemed to leave westbound Twenty-Fifth with too little traffic to notice. In the people storm of New York City, Twenty-Fifth was usually another of those countless eyes of relative peace.

"Without God, everything is permitted," Brian said. Usually when he said that, and he said it fairly often, the emphasis was on "God." This time it was on "Everything."

That night the block between Eighth and Ninth Avenue was thickly crowded and echoing with the voices of broken youth, and there were flashes of colored dresses between black suits. A boy in a khaki blazer was balancing on an iron railing and three girls were encouraging his stunt. Two women, older than most of the crowd, were waltzing hand in hand as they whistled the Blue Danube in unison. Beside a stoop near the middle of the long block, a pair of wingtips tapped around the swish of a ruffled dress. A skateboard rumbled and then clacked up upon stopping. Laughter crackled from a semicircle of black and white and skin and hair. The sober prom of 2005 was moving and growing.

Brian twitched his right hand in the direction of the throng. "Forgive them, for they know not what they do."

"I wash my hands of this game," I said.

"Vanity, vanity – all is vanity and a chasing of the wind," Brian said.

We neared the crowd, and an arm of approaching men extended from the blob of people and pulled us into the pulsing body of kids. The Saturday night Sunday school was over. There was that feeling felt at the best of times in Alcoholics Anonymous, the feeling of unity despite bizarrely disparate members. Smiles fostered smiles, yellow and white flashes of teeth. Slaps hit my back and stung. A girl flicked my ass with her finger and then fled to a hiding spot behind a stoop's wide railing. Two motorcycles roared up and the conversations got louder and stayed louder even after two leather men stopped roaring their engines. Enveloped by the buzz of talk and laughter, I still couldn't give myself over to the joy of the night.

There was intense grief for loss that had yet to come. The best of my life was already falling away. That would be my last night with these New Yorkers who took me in and loved me for the mess I was, and my last night in a city that consumes ebullience as if it were bubbles in champagne. I wanted to grasp at the suits and dresses as if they could hold me fast to my city. I looked over the magazine's worth of haircuts to the sky beyond even New Jersey and thought of apple blossoms. My life was falling away like so many petals and I could only hope it would yet bear fruit.

Dry World

Brian slapped my back as a looked at a girl. "You know what my sponsor says? The beaver trail leads to wine country."

"There's lots of slips behind this many skirts," I said.

I noticed a blond in a wedding dress standing alone at the western edge of the crowd. It looked as though there was no one between her and the horizon. A warm gust passed through her hair but it barely moved. I assumed it was weighted down with styling products. The skirt of her dress only hung to her knees, and was translucent, letting a second tighter, shorter skirt be seen. Her feet were bare and there were white, stubbed heels dangling from her right fingers. At last she flashed her face and I saw Billie in a wig. Her face shone in half silhouette. She threw so much joy my way that I check to see who else was around. There, directly behind me, in seersucker and a straw hat, burning as hot as the little cigar in his hand, was Roger approaching. It could not be known at whom she smiled. I suppose she was taking care of two with only one look. I smelled peach smoke and felt a meaty paw on my shoulder, and Roger and I were both there.

"You look like heaven on the outside and hell on the inside," said Roger.

"I can't work for you anymore," I said.

"You really going to let a thin skirt get between you and the future?" Roger asked.

There is a scene in Roger's most successful novel, the only one they made into a movie, where a woman takes off all white underwear and waves them like a flag. I thought of the shot from the film, where the light is blown out and white and Kate Winslet smiles so wide that she looks like a feeding shark and you want to get eaten. Billie was smiling that same way at us, and I thought she must have been mad to feel comfortable with her two suitors together conferring. Yet that is how she looked, joyous, and that was also what made Billie so attractive at times – her apparent release from worry about possessiveness. There is vicarious joy to be taken from someone who is shameless. It opens possibilities, but also invites danger.

Brian joined me on the edge of the crowd, tapping the shoulder he wasn't behind to let me know he was near. I looked at him, and he looked at me with intense fealty. I knew he would go to any lengths for me. It was as clear as his eyes. There was in them a fanaticism seen in photographs of mujahedeen. In a way I didn't yet realize, Brian had made me the higher power that kept him sober. His mind was misfiring enough that this faith drove him to his doom. It was, on my part, an accident, no matter what has been inferred since. All I did was play a song. He was the one who claimed it had a secret message in it telling him to kill.

Playing music is what I do, if at all possible, when I get into an uncomfortable social situation. This has nothing to do with impressing people, though I have been accused of being so motivated. Music is something I need to do, and the time I need to most is when I feel awkward. I couldn't imagine a stranger position than the one I was in with Billie and Roger, and so I fled in search of a piano. I felt there had to be one at the elementary school that was hosting the prom. It took several minutes but I found one under a blue plastic tarp, the kind used to gather suburban leaves. I thought of my home and knew I would be back in the world of yard work soon. The emotions in me were as jumbled as a crossword without a list of clues. There seemed to be a pattern, but I could not discern it though the chaos of ignorance.

The keys moved and worked, I was glad to feel. I didn't bother to warm up. Instead I played a song I had written about a dying young. As I played and sang, I felt the footsteps of a very heavy man behind me and knew it was Brian. This was his favorite song. He would sing one of its lines repeatedly: Watch for falling rockers.

After the song, he looked at me longingly. We were passing toward and away from each other even then, our bond strengthening before it broke. His face churned up some tears with its twists. He would miss me dearly. I could read it on him like one of his tattoos. The light in that back room caught the dust in the air, and there was a shaft from a streetlamp showing the air as it might were it snowing. As with the tarp I was taken back to Michigan, watching the winter through my bedroom window. I could escape thoughts of where I couldn't escape.

Brian's face changed then. His eyes went blank, staring at a point of infinite distance. With that spacey stare, he flatly said something I misinterpreted. I still grasp at that mistake as if I could unmake it through the cruel fondling of misfortunes that is at best regret. He said, "Thank you for telling me what to do." It made sense on a level that proved to be deception. I had told Brian what to do dozens of times. As his sponsor, it was, in a way, my charge. There seemed nothing strange about what he had said and yet, because of what he did next, I find the strangeness in it now. I see

the blankness to his affect, how he has dissociated and is in the
grips of a psychotic puppeteer. I want to believe there is a string I
could have pulled that might have kept him from his hideous crime,
but I am no more the puppeteer than Woland was. I believe we
have choices. I have to. The alternative shirks personal
responsibility and leaves me empty. It makes me feel too good and
too bad about myself at once. No, Brian chose to do what he did.

I was halfway through a second song when I heard the
screams, dozens of them, and shouts, too, shouts of "No!" and
"Stop!" By the time I got to the street there was nothing left of
Roger Abbey's neck except for weakening pulses of red. Brian had
stabbed Roger several times. Brian's dress was streaked in red in a
way that made it look as though the coloration were just some bold
stroke of fashion. Parts of Roger flowed into the gutter, and the rest
laid under Billie crying silently. She closed his eyelids and kissed
each of them.

The Siberian knife of walrus ivory hung in the air, Brian's
hand aloft. Brian refused to turn it over. I know now that he wanted
to kill himself but lacked the courage, and also knew that that
courage no longer had to come from him. But the police didn't
shoot him dead as Brian probably thought they would. When they
got there, Brian lost a kneecap and was hauled off by four officers.
It took that many to carry his flailing, weeping form into the car.

The devil was among the detectives who came later. He
stepped out of the back of a squad car through a door that didn't
open. As he stood he stared at me and winked one blue-gold eye,
and then the other. Somehow they sparkled in the low light. There
were other colors and shines. The paleness of Roger's seersucker

showed a bib of blood, while the rest of it rotated in its coloration, shifting in time with the sirens.

The police had a list of questions that blur together now like words read by an old man without bifocals. This myopia of memory, the same one that let me forget the pain of Gisele and then kill things with Billie, is the core of the alcoholic sickness. It lets us make mistakes over and over again and never learn a lesson from them. We drink and we love like this and we love like this even after drinking. Yet there are times when it is good to forget, and I am grateful every bit of that night I don't remember. There are too many memories of the death already.

Only when Roger's body was seized by paramedics did Woland approach. He took off his skull cap and revealed stripes of salty hair across a bare scalp. I shuddered, not knowing if it was from shock or cold. He offered me a drink and I declined.

A breeze off the Hudson was shuffling the young heads of thin trees. The gloaming had passed and night had cast the buildings in black and blue, but the sky was the brown of white bread crust. More of the windows in these building were glowing than at dusk, and a crescent moon hung in the west like a hook that could carry all the dreams of earth. I only wondered if it could bear the night terrors.

There was a long pause where I looked at the devil as I might look at my twin, communicating wordlessly our mutual understanding. The specter looked through me then, as he said. "I remember Sumer, that first drink of alcohol, those first cuneiform. I love writers. I love all would-be gods." Woland took his first step into the air. He walked up the beam of a streetlamp, straining at the incline as if he were climbing one of those steep dunes rolling behind our home in Roosevelt. When he reached its peak, he grabbed the crescent moon hanging and swung himself up from it as might a child on a jungle gym. I was sure he would fall. There were few stars to see. But he grabbed one, he grabbed Mars, and hung from that dry world as if it were a lifeline.

Chapter 24

Gambling Body's Beating Parts

Michigan

Foam broke through the blue background. Its waves held a steady hiss that rose once or twice a minute toward a rumble, but never quite got loud. Above it hung gobs of gray that broke into a strip of clear sky just above the water. The sun was moving through this strip fast enough to notice. It was Japanese flag whose colors had run in a wash. It was dusk.

Sixteen circles of white dotted my green backyard. Linen tablecloths hung around the edges of tables. Blue circles of delftware dotted this whiteness. There were delicate arrangements of blue orchids in their centers. Silver around the plates had a hundred year's worth of slight, fought-against tarnish on them. Precisely engraved place cards cast shadows a foot long.

Under a purple sky pink monkeys made nice. Male chins were smooth and moving to make clever noises. Most of the necks were exposed, but one-third were still surrounded by white, pointed collars. Some of those points opened onto undershirts, some onto skin. Hair puffed out of some of these white edges. Seven women jostled curves under French silk the color of the sky, somewhere between pink and lavender. Each of their necks were spotted with pearls. Below the pearls, strapless push-up bras shifted in and out of view. Bare shoulders ran downhill to hands that followed old etiquette.

Rudely I stood observing the wedding reception at the edge of the yard. I held my drink over the sun and blocked its redness. My other hand took a cigarette in for a pull from my mouth. The band was between a song, and I could hear the paper of my smoke crackle and the ice cubes in my black Russian tinkle. I wondered at the silence, pronounced even for a pause in the set. I scanned the muted crowd, and behind black the gate to the driveway I saw Gisele.

The movements she made felt slowed down in the manner of a car accident. I anticipated that the next moments could dangerously change the rest of my life. Her sundress shuffled around her thighs, blown by a gust off the lake. Gisele wore a pattern of white and pale blue that reminded me of my family's delftware. She might have matched the occasion well were it not for her reputation.

I heard dozens of hushed words at once, hissing like air out of a tire. My parents had told the story of my bloody dawn arrival to enough people that it seemed like nearly every guest had head a word of John Rook's violently psychotic fiancé. Considering how dramatic the response of the stunned onlookers you might have thought that my parents had distributed photographs to every table. Apparently whispers were doing something almost as drastic. I wasn't sure if my perception of this silence were grandiose paranoia or dramatic fact. Perhaps it was somewhere in between. Quickly I looked back to my family's table, where my parents were smiling weakly, in that way that parents smile when they are unhappy with what makes a child happy but still happy that the child is happy.

Dry World

I set my drink on the railing, dropped my burning cigarette off the edge of the dune, and wove through the tables, jogging until she was in my arms. Inside them she moved strangely, twisting slightly and shuddering, and I knew something serious was the matter. Yet she didn't push me away, and her eyes held flickers of the old passion in the corners and reflections. There was probably something amiss in the way my embrace felt. I loved but did not trust her. Still, my mind was already apologizing for twisted moves she had yet to make. I was in another abusive relationship, and this one was romantic. I took her left hand and thumbed my family's ring. She was wearing it. We were engaged. I wanted her so badly and so badly wanted her to be happy. I held back out of fear of what she'd do to me.

"Let's go somewhere private," Gisele said. There was a flatness to her voice that made it impossible for me to read. I couldn't tell whether she wanted to screw or screw me up.

"The yard is full. The beach is full. The house is full, except for the attic," I said.

"Let's go there."

The cover band began. I was expected to be there for the father-daughter dance but I was walking away from that family obligation. No one bothered to stop me, perhaps out of fear of Gisele or me or both. I was known to be the mad member of the family and many distant relatives treated me with a mixture condescension and placation. They wanted to keep the mad man happy so he didn't go mad yet again. My escape from where I was supposed to be came as no surprise. I later learned that they had a replacement for me lined up so that my bridesmaid didn't dance alone. Then, though, then Gisele was everything.

Together we passed through the white French doors whose lock I could always pick, past the couch where I lay for days during my first breakdown, up the stairs where pictures of my brothers and me hung in chronological order, past the study containing the books I'd bought on binges, through a squeaky white door and a creaky flight of stairs that always made it hard to sneak out as a teenager, to the safest place I knew. I closed the windows and put on our music, an album of carrot-flower kings we had listened to on our first night together. Gisele burst into tears. I held her huddling shake as she pounded my chest with her head as if it were a piston firing the engine of a car that could no longer steer. There had always been something wrong with her, but that something felt irreparable. I could feel it in her shudders, I could feel it in her sobs, so I asked, during a storm-eye when all we heard was music, this: "What's the matter, darling?"

"Tom and Chloe," she said. "They're together. Or they hooked up. I know they did."

"The wedding went well," I said. "I sang a good song."

Gisele pushed me away and walked toward the window overlooking the backyard. She reopened what I'd just shut, and the classic rock boomed in from a makeshift stage. The mash-up of my rock and Paul's rock fell strangely in sync: both songs happened to be in the key of F and the two became one tune. Over this strange commingling of genres, she pushed her mouth into my ear so I could hear her. The smell of her hair, that lavender smell, buried me in snapshots from out time together. In my reverie she told me that Tom and Chloe had bonded over their hatred of me. I went to shut the window that I might hear her better and she grabbed my arm hard and frighteningly. Stopped from quieting the attic, I could still hear her scream. She shrieked, and then: "My ex-boyfriend is fucking your ex-girlfriend because of that fucking book."

This is the cruel truth of words: they can't be unsaid; they can't be unread.

I said, "I'm happy for them."

The attic was the size of the entire first two stories. The floorboards were dingy oak that hadn't been stained in decades. Its ceiling was high, but at its edges it sloped except at the four windows facing the front and back of the house. Even with these inclines, I could stand upright at the lowest point of them. Gisele began to pace the edge of the back wall, stopping once to look out the window, and then went back to pacing again. From her face and her agitation, I could tell that because of what I'd said, everything within her had just gotten worse. At last she stopped and looked at me with weary eyes, the kind of eyes seen in paintings of saints.

As she was fingering the ring, my mind flashed back to the cutting impact of her punch. Her thin arms were deceptively strong. With her short and thin fingers barely holding the ring at all, that band came off easily. She crossed the floorboards, the hard soles of her flats knocking on the oak planks. I could sense the pressure of her approach. Wood floors are like that. I felt her gently take and stroke open my hand, and then I felt cold white gold in my palm and the poke of a diamond pebble. "Take it," she said, "in remembrance of me."

It was over. It was ironic that I didn't expect as much. I was somehow in shock. There was nothing in me or on me, there was only numbness. I still felt nothing as she walked over to the stereo and skipped it to the disc's last track. I felt that if I let myself feel, feelings would kill me.

As I fought to stay shocked, the breeze twisted her small sundress. With the last of the sun behind it, I could see the red shine through the thin fabric covering the distance between her thighs. There was the first woman I had ever had. Her posture was taut and high. She had always been proud. Within everyone there is a place no one can touch, a place of hope and peace. It is our gyroscope, guiding us on our flight through its perpetual balance. I want to believe this, just as I wanted to believe then that that place would allow my love to find a safe landing.

Gisele reached out then, reached for something in the sky. Her arm had no sleeve, and her skin was so pale for a summer that it could have been on a hermit. Her mouth moved then, and with all the noise I could tell whether she spoke softly or only mouthed the words, but either way I knew she was talking to herself alone. It looked as though she were trying wish on a star. The only ones I could see were Venus and Mars and the Dog Star. Then she went out the window.

Just like our room in O' Neill, there was a trapezoidal balcony above a window box on the second floor. Gisele had headed out and was just barely sinking into the soft tar of an old roof. I badly wanted a cigarette and decided to join her out there. I climbed out, and in my tux sat Indian style on shingles still warm from the hot day. When she dropped her hand from its reach, I knew she was about to say goodbye. I would wait to smoke until she did. But she only stood in the billow of a pale blue dress, she stood, and then she sang along with the record. "God is the place you will wait for the rest of your life."

When she jumped, headfirst, screams rose from the crowd. I heard my mother's voice, and I heard my father's voice, and I heard Jim Harrison laugh loudly. She landed on a pot of geraniums, snapping her spine at the neck and dying instantly. There she lay, dead in the center of a gathering crowd, yellow flowers tangled in her yellow hair.

I stayed where I was, watching the afterglow of the sunset fade from the reddening ledges of clouds, watching the tip of my cigarette illuminate the darkening spring evening as my father called for me to come down. For an instant, I thought of taking his orders and twisting them like a dagger. I thought of taking the fast way down. But then a strange confidence filled me, and I felt loved, and I knew that I would never kill myself. I felt I could see the end of my life and it would not end as Gisele's had. I come back to that moment on the tarry trapezoid whenever I get depressed. Every time, the same kind of thread that pulled me to the V-Tree guides me to safety and solace. I found and still find the gyroscope.

My father was angry and yelling at the best man. It seemed as though Jim Harrison's laughter never ended. My mother was ushering guests back to their seats. George was on a cell phone calling 911. The crowd rumbled behind it all.

It was then that I saw Woland passing through the crowd and through the French doors. After a minute with little suspense, he did what I knew he would. He emerged from the attic window and sat beside me in his loose gray suit, kicking his legs as if he were on a playground swing. Into the silk shoulder of his jacket I sobbed. I heard him light a cigarette. He blew smoke into my ear as he asked me, softly, "Would you like some vodka now?" I took a long drink, one of my last. I would quit the next day. When I lifted my head, Venus was gone and Mars had risen over the horizon, bright as it was that whole hateful summer of 2003 that followed. To myself I mouthed a line of mine: All I feel is what's real. Then I looked to my family and they glared at me, and, just at my lowest point, a cardinal landed beside the corpse.

Dry World is a GenZ Publishing Book

GenZ™ is an innovative publisher for the new generation to have their work seen, recognized, published and read by millions. When an individual is chosen to be published on GenZ™, they can use that experience in their portfolios, for résumés, to share with friends, family, and fans. It is an accomplishment to be proud of for the rest of their lives.

We are on a mission to improve the world one word at a time. That is why we are the place for voices to be heard in a way not previously done in print and on digital media. It is a way to support young writers, our new voices.

It can be nearly impossible for young writers with promising talent to produce standout work that will be recognized, because of the state of the publishing and digital media industries. Having work recognized in a sea of so many writers is even tougher. That is why there is an underrepresentation of young and innovative voices in the publishing and print world. There are many unheard voices. GenZ is on a mission to change that.

GenZ™ provides a medium where these people can be positively recognized for their work through a professional product and supportive company.

Learn more about GenZ Publishing, how you can get involved, and all of our newest releases at GenZPublishing.org. Like us on Facebook at GenZ Publishing and follow us on Twitter @GenZPub.

Acknowledgments

Personally, I never would have succeeded without care from my wife, my family, and the following exceptional people: Andrew and Lynn Salvage, Kha Ngo, Thomas Leary, James Bray, Arthur Brickman, Donald Moss, Eugene Goldberg, Carol Friar, and the entire staff of Community Mental Health in Muskegon, Michigan.

I need to thank Ian Link, Brett Karis, and Eric Goldart for listening and contributing to the writing of the lyrics in this novel and the development of the songs supporting them.

I also need to acknowledge the writers who reviewed some or all of this manuscript and helped it become what it is: Samuel Neis, Kathryn Harrison, Colum McCann, Jeffrey Rotter, Colson Whitehead, Walter Mosley, Andrew Sean Greer, Patricia O'Dowd, and Benjamin Evans. Special thanks go to Peter Carey who has generously supported all of my work and carefully humored me since 2004.

Finally, thank you to anyone who has listened to me talk about my writing or writing in general, including employers, co-workers, colleagues, students, teachers, and sympathizers yet to be mentioned.

None of your kindness is forgotten and I am grateful to you all.

About Dylan James Brock

Dylan Brock was born in Michigan. He was educated at the University of Michigan in Ann Arbor starting at age sixteen, and completed a fiction writing MFA at Hunter College in New York City in 2006.

During graduate school, Dylan was concurrently occupied as a singer songwriter with frequent stints at CBGBs until it closed in 2005. In 2006 he founded Jumberlack, a record label that went on to have ten releases by Michigan and New York City artists.

Starting in early 2011, Dylan was fiction editor of the arts review Fogged Clarity, where he worked for just over a year. In 2016 *Dry World* was accepted for publication by GenZ. This novel is written around a 25 song cycle of original recorded music available at **dylanjamesbrock.com**

www.ingramcontent.com/pod-product-compliance
Lightning Source LLC
Chambersburg PA
CBHW021116260626
47169CB00012B/2162